VISION QUEST

Books by Pamela F. Service

VISION QUEST

Pamela F. Service

A Jean Karl book

ATHENEUM   1989   NEW YORK

Atheneum
Macmillan Publishing Company
866 Third Avenue, New York, NY 10022
Collier Macmillan Canada, Inc.
First Edition
Printed in the United States of America
10 9 8 7 6 5 4 3 2 1

Designed by Barbara A. Fitzsimmons

Library of Congress Cataloging-in-Publication Data
Service, Pamela F.
Vision quest/Pamela F. Sevice.—1st. ed.   p.   cm.
"A Jean Karl book."
Summary: Kate finds life dreary in her small Nevada desert town until contact with an Indian artifact sends her visions of a restless shaman from the past, visions which eventually drag her and her friend Jimmy Fong into that far distant Nevada.
ISBN 0-689-31498-1
1.Indians of North America—Juvenile fiction.   [1. Space and time—Fiction.   2. Indians of North America—Fiction.
3. Nevada—Fiction.]   I. Title.
PZ7.S4885Vi   1989
[Fic]—dc19
88–27486   CIP   AC

*For Forrest LeRoy Horner
and for cousin W. U. G.*

VISION QUEST

ONE

DESPITE THE HEAT, SHE FELT A COLD JAB OF FEAR, cold as the snake's unblinking stare. Scarcely a foot away, it coiled on the sun-warmed rock like some ancient piece of jewelry—a treasure worked in deadly coppery patterns.

At first Kate had only heard it. That dry, sharp rattle had been new to her, a sound like seedpods shaken in an angry wind. Yet she had known it at once. And now, fear spurted through her like venom, leaving her numb and frozen.

Motionless, the girl and the snake stared at each other. A silent shadow swept over them. The rattler struck then, not at Kate but toward a crevice in a protective tumble of rocks. Kate looked up. A large bird glided low overhead. It had missed its meal of basking snake, but it would find another. With two mighty flaps of its wings, it rose above the enclosing cliff and soared out of sight.

Kate looked down again. The snake was only a glint among shadowy rocks. She breathed a trembling sigh; then, as if a spell had broken, she turned and ran. With

1

fear-sharpened sight, she scanned the way ahead. Scattered pebbles, dry wind-curdled dust, sun-bleached rocks—all could hide some coiled or crouching threat.

Fear pumped through her until she reached the ragged shade of a pinyon pine. Grabbing the reassuring roughness of its trunk, she stumbled to a halt and took several deep breaths.

"Okay," she announced shakily, "all you snakes, scorpions, and other nasties, clear out. I'm sitting down."

She slumped onto a broad, sloping rock. Slowly fear drained away, leaving her weak and trembling.

"Thanks, Uncle Bernie," she said into the hot, dry silence. "Go out and get to know the land, you say. I do, and it almost kills me."

She shivered, involuntarily rerunning the scene in her mind. The rattle, the deadly coil, the sudden shadow.

Again, she looked up at the cliff tops, now empty and silent, shimmering with afternoon heat. That had sure been a huge bird. Some sort of hawk? Maybe even an eagle. Kind of exciting, she had to admit. Well, maybe if the land had almost killed her, it had also sent the bird to save her.

She snorted. This dry, bitter land didn't give a darn about her. And frankly, the feeling was mutual. She stood up and glared around her. The land glared back with intense, bright heat.

Slowly now, Kate walked on, cautiously scanning the rocks ahead. What a sad joke. All those years of wanting a permanent home, then ending up with this!

2

VISION QUEST

Her life had been one military base after another. She'd just start to know a place, its trees and weather, the house and new school, she'd just start to make friends, when, pow, they'd be off again. Her dad had a new assignment. They'd pull up roots and start again somewhere else.

Silly kid that she'd been, she'd thought that if they just had a permanent home somewhere, all their troubles would end. And then the worst trouble of all had come along. It had given them a home but far too late to do any good.

The stark landscape blurred around her as she thought about it for the millionth time. Her dad sent to the Middle East. Her wonderful dad, pointlessly dead, their life shattered, no more home for her and her mom on military bases. Then her mom's uncle Bernie's offer. He had a home for them, but what a home. This!

Stuffing wisps of brown hair back into her ponytail, Kate stared again at the landscape, feeling as desolate as it looked. At her feet, the dirt was a dry ashy brown, scattered with pebbles and ants. It stretched in all directions, naked except for an occasional scraggly pine or clump of gray-green sage. The sun battered everything into colorless silence, and the very air smelled hot, dry, and empty.

Coming at last to the faint dirt road, she jumped with alarm, then let out her breath in relief. The scuttling gray shape was only a tumbleweed. She watched as the wind, furnace-hot and dry, jerked the rootless tangle along the road and then, with a sudden gust, snared it in a barbed-wire fence.

That was her, Kate decided—rootless and aimless. And for her, the end of the trip, the rusty barbed wire, was Argentum, Nevada.

Dejectedly, Kate plodded along the dusty track toward her new home. Skirting a bluff, she saw it before her. Its single paved street, an old state highway, cut steeply up a narrow valley toward a craggy mountain pass.

Over a century ago, Argentum had been a bustling silver town. Saloons, assay offices, and scores of thriving businesses had lined this street. Some of the square false-fronts still stood, but many of the buildings behind them were dilapidated and empty. The population had steadily dwindled until a few years ago, when one of the old mines had reopened, bringing a modest new influx of people.

Kate followed her track until it came out at the base of Juniper Street, the name given the road for the short space that it ran through town. She sighed. Being out in the wild was bad enough, but being back in "civilization" was almost worse. Trudging up the street, she decided she wouldn't tell her mom or Uncle Bernie about the rattlesnake. That could mean that Uncle Bernie's adjustment plan for her "getting to know the land" might be scrapped in favor of her mother's far more repellent idea of getting to know the people.

She didn't want to know the people, she thought. She didn't want to make friends. Actually, it seemed she didn't even know how to anymore.

As she walked along, she could still see them, her friends at all those other homes. Sarah and Eileen and

Sissy. And way back, curly-haired, dimply Maggie. They'd been best friends. And it had been the same with every one of them. Tearful farewells. Promises to remember each other forever. Then the letters coming less and less frequently as the one left behind found new friends and forgot.

Kate stumbled on a loose chunk of sidewalk. They can't even make sidewalks around here, she thought bitterly, looking ahead to where crumbling concrete gave way to a stretch of worn wooden planking.

Then her stomach tightened. Two girls were coming out of Nel's, the town's main store—Stephanie and Paula, popular, bubbly, local girls. Kate had sat next to Paula in English, the first few months they'd been here before school closed for the summer. She'd seemed a nice enough girl, but Kate had hardly been able to make herself say two words to her, and after a while Paula seemed to stop expecting it. Now Kate just wanted to become invisible.

As the girls stepped out, their gaze swept over her, and they continued talking and walking up the street. Kate realized then that she needn't bother with invisibility. She'd done such a good job of avoiding people that they'd practically stopped noticing her.

Well, that's the way she wanted it! If you weren't close to people, it couldn't hurt to lose them. She walked on up the street, but her defiance quavered a little around the edges. Looking up, she saw the museum and changed course toward it. Her mom would be there, and suddenly Kate wanted familiar, untrying company.

VISION QUEST

Years ago, the old jail house had been turned into a storehouse for the town's memorabilia. The collection of artifacts had been halfheartedly organized and irregularly opened to the public. In recent years, it had been closed altogether, but when Kate's mother had moved to town, her uncle had persuaded the town officials to give her a part-time job as museum curator. After all, she had a degree in history—French history, admittedly—but she was anxious to have something to do and was willing to work for a token salary.

Eagerly now Kate crossed the quiet street and hurried toward the old two-story building. The bright sun showed up all the cracks and chinks in the plaster, but she knew that inside the thick brick walls, it would be cool.

Kate slowed as she neared the building, frowning at the big, dusty van parked in front. It was black and hand painted with a bizarre splash of red and gold flames. Not a local. Probably summer tourists in search of the Old West. It was to attract them and their money that the old museum had been reopened. Hesitantly Kate opened the door. She didn't want to walk into a bevy of strangers.

Blinking in the cool dimness, she looked around. No one was in the entry hall, but she could hear voices in the next room. She peeped in. Mrs. Elliot was seated at a table across from a large redheaded man. The contents of a cardboard box were spread between them. Kate wanted to slip away but was curious about what was on the table. Quietly she walked up.

The man had a big belly, a bushy red beard, and a

6

wreath of red hair around a shiny bald spot. Kate thought he looked like a younger Santa Claus, though she didn't sense anything particularly jolly about him.

He looked up as Kate approached, smiled blandly, and went back to pulling rocks and clay pots out of the box. Her mother smiled more warmly.

"Ah, Kate, come look. This gentleman has brought some old Indian tools and pottery he thinks the museum might be interested in buying."

Kate did want to see but did not want to talk to the man. As she stepped hesitantly to the table, she hoped he would ignore her. He did, totally.

"You won't find a better private collection anywhere, Mrs. Elliot. And my prices are very reasonable. You buy any or all of this material, and your museum board will consider it a wise investment."

Mrs. Elliot laughed nervously. "I really do doubt that. As I said, we're just starting to get this museum on its feet, and the Board has given me no money to buy anything for the collection. Indian things aren't my specialty, but I'm sure some of these are very nice. I just haven't a penny to buy them with."

"Ah, but with your museum trying to upgrade itself, that's when you need a really first-class Indian collection. It'd catch the tourists like flypaper."

"Yes, maybe it would. But I've just started here, and I hardly know what Indian things we already have. And, anyway, I really, truly don't have any acquisition money."

The big man sighed theatrically and began picking up the painted pots and stone tools. "Well, Mrs. Elliot, it's too bad, it really is. This is a fine opportunity you're passing up here."

She said nothing as he continued packing, his large hands remarkably careful with the fragile artifacts. He continued heavily, "It is a shame, but maybe once you give it some thought, you'll change your mind. I doubt your old collection has material as fine as some of this. And this is just a sample, mind. I have much more and better in the van."

He slapped down the lid of the cardboard box. Mrs. Elliot stood up. "I don't know about changing my mind, but thank you for coming by."

"Yep. Maybe next time I'm through town, your Board'll have loosened the purse strings a little— though lots of the best pieces could be sold by then. I do quite a brisk business, you know. Can't give you a card, I'm afraid. I'm always on the move. But you won't find a better collector and dealer in the state than old honest Pete. Ask anyone."

Mrs. Elliot politely ushered the dealer out the main door, then returned to the workroom. "What a slime."

"Yeah," Kate agreed. "He reminds me of those guys who sell knife sets and furniture on TV. But I thought the Board had given you some money to buy things with. If there was something really neat, I mean."

"Sure they did, a little. But I'm not going to deal with his kind. Honest Pete, ha! He's a pothunter, plain and simple."

"A pothunter?"

"People who dig up old sites looking for pots or stone tools or other things they can sell to collectors and curio shops. They make big bucks but mess up the sites so much that scientists can't learn a thing from them. It's not legal, but nobody much stops them. Pothunters make me sick."

She went back to the table to straighten up papers pushed aside for the demonstration. "Rats! That man forgot one of his stone tools. I don't want any part of this. Here, Kate, he may still be around. Run out and return it to him, will you?"

"Me?"

"Come on, little Miss Shy Flower. It won't kill you to walk up to him and say, 'You forgot this.'"

She plunked a black stone into Kate's hand. It had a nice feeling, heavy and smooth, but that didn't help much with the tightness in her stomach at having to go talk to a stranger.

"Go on now," her mother said, "before he leaves."

Kate trudged to the door and stepped out. The black van with the painted flames was gone. But her surge of relief was short-lived. Squinting down the street, she saw it parked a block away in front of one of the town's two saloons. Resigned, she walked toward it.

Her heart felt cold and heavy, like the stone in her hand. He'd probably gone in to have a drink. People weren't so strict around here about minors going into bars if they had a message or something. But if she did, people would turn and look at her; maybe the bartender or the slot-machine players would say something witty. No way. She'd just stay out here until old honest Pete came out.

Retreating to the shade of a derelict building next

door, Kate sat on the edge of the plank sidewalk and waited. Idly she turned the stone over in her hands. A dull black stone about three inches long, it had been ground into a smooth tapered cylinder. The stone lay cool and soothing in her hand, and she liked its feeling of weight.

She held it up to the daylight. Its smooth black surface was marked with a groove. Starting at one tapered end, it spiraled around the thickened center and down to the other thin tip. She ran a finger along the smooth spiral path, then up and back again several times.

It was pretty neat to think how old this thing was, to think that some Indian, some other person, had once made it, once held it in his hand. She wondered what he had been like. Maybe he'd had troubles, too, maybe people had left him, forgotten him. Crouching here in the shade, she could almost see him doing the same all those years ago. Almost see him holding the same stone in his hand, reaching out toward her.

She blinked. A little too much imagination there. But still, it was a nice stone, well made, whoever had done it. Again she ran a finger slowly along the spiral groove. Somehow it felt right. A line that went on and on, never really ending. Just holding it was almost a link to the person who'd made it. A comforting sort of link.

A sweet, beery smell wafted through the dry air. Kate looked up to see the big red-haired man standing beside his van, fumbling in a pocket for his keys.

Guiltily she jumped up. But what a crime to give this wonderful stone to that boor. She slipped it into her pocket and turned to walk away. He'd probably never miss it.

Still, this was a looted artifact, sort of stolen property. She'd better not keep it, even if he really had no more right to it than she did.

Weighed with more than her usual shyness, she retrieved the stone and took a few steps towards the van. Words jammed in her throat.

"Excuse me," she finally managed.

The man spun around with a very un-Santa Claus-like glare.

"Excuse me, but you left this at the museum."

He looked down, then smiled broadly. "Why, so I did. A good piece, too. Found it way out in the desert, all by its lonesome. Must've been lying there for thousands of years. Fetch a fat price, that one will. Good for holding down papers."

Chortling, he reached out his large, stubby hand, and Kate almost snatched her own hand away. She had a wild desire to run off, clutching the stone and its link to some ancient world.

He grabbed it from her. She jerked back, and a bright light flashed in her eyes. Sun, maybe, reflecting off a window across the street. It left her blinded for a moment, seeing swirling patterns of light.

When she could see again, the man had already climbed into the van and was starting the engine. Trembling, Kate stepped back into the shade. Through a dazzling afterimage of spiraling lights, she watched the van back out and rumble down the street. Suddenly she could have cried from loss.

TWO

FOR SEVERAL MINUTES, IT SEEMED, KATE STOOD empty and alone, staring down the vacant street. Then she shook herself like a dog shakes off water. What was the matter with her? It was just a stone, not even hers. How could its loss hurt so much? No answer came. And suddenly very tired, she began trudging home.

Argentum had been built in such a narrow valley that only the highway could fit into the bottom of the cleft. The other streets, all gravel, had to cling to the steep mountains on either side. The older—once grand—houses perched precariously over the main street, their backs built right into the rocky mountainsides. In one spot near the bottom of the town, a side valley joined the other. The resulting wide space was dotted with new mobile homes, the school, and gravelly mounds marking old mines.

Kate was still trying to shake the odd feeling of loss as she climbed her own one-block-long street. The sight of the huge red and blue poppies in Uncle Bernie's garden helped. They looked as if they'd been made of tissue paper by a color-mad kindergartener.

In fact, she reflected, looking beyond the weathered picket fence, all of Uncle Bernie's place was a sort of visual madhouse. Under the shifting shade of aspen and cottonwood, the garden had so many stone niches and terraces that it resembled a miniature ruined city. And amid garish flowers and plump green succulents stood plaster deer, phony Greek statues, sundials, bird-baths, and an enormous concrete frog. Cascading down the side of a porch were sprays of half-wild yellow roses. Kate had never imagined that so many blossoms could be crammed on one unkempt plant.

The house looked equally crazy. The front part had been built of brick in Argentum's heyday. Since then, it had been added on to many times in wood, stone, and cinder block until it grew out of the hillside like some exotic mountain temple in *National Geographic.* It was certainly a contrast to the tidy, efficient, military houses she'd always lived in. Her uncle—or, rather, great-uncle—who wrote books about the West, had lived here since he was a boy, and Kate thought he was rather like his house—strange, disorganized, and oddly appealing.

His gravelly voice greeted her the moment the screen door slammed behind her. "Ah, the explorer returneth." She turned to see his gray bird nest of hair rising from the gloom of the cellar stairs. In moments, he was standing in the center of the kitchen, tanned, hairy arms wrapped around a large cardboard box that clanked as he placed it on the floor.

"Thought I'd clean up some of my bottle collection.

Then maybe I'll donate some to your mom's museum. Ought to share the wealth, you know." He reached in and pulled out a dark, dust-grimed bottle. "Come on, let's give 'em a good scrubbing. Some are as pretty as jewels once the sun comes through 'em."

He turned on the tap and liberally squirted dish detergent into one side of the double sink. "So, what did you see out there?"

"Oh, rocks, sand, and sagebrush mostly." Handing him the bottles, Kate decided she definitely wouldn't mention snakes. But there was something else. "And I saw a really enormous bird. I mean *big*. It sort of glided below some cliffs, then just a couple of flaps took it over. Really big wings. Do you have any eagles around here?"

"Well, that could've been a hawk, but for a couple of years now, there's been a pair of eagles nesting not too far from here. Up by Indian Cliffs."

Indians. Something else she wasn't sure she wanted to mention. But then, why not? The stone was gone. Again she was gripped by that sharp sense of loss, and she hurried to say something, anything, to fill the emptiness.

"Speaking of Indians, there was a slimy guy in the museum just now trying to sell Mom some old Indian stuff. She sent him packing and got all huffy about his being a pothunter. He . . . he left one of his stones behind."

She plunged a sudsy hand into her jeans pocket, then stopped, confused. She'd given the thing back. For a moment, though, it had seemed as if she'd felt it

14

there. Crazy. She glanced sideways, but Uncle Bernie hadn't noticed. He was scrubbing and lecturing on pothunters.

"Of course, they're pothunters and pothunters, but the type that tear apart old places and desecrate graves just to make a fast buck, they get my goat. Smart of your mom to give him the brush-off. Now, look at that, will you? Could've been carved out of amethyst, that could."

He held a sparkling purple bottle up to the sunny window. "Found some around old mining camps, but a lot came from our own town dump. You can date 'em by the shape of the mouth and how far down the mold marks come."

When Kate's mother came home, the two bottle scrubbers were evicted from the kitchen while she made dinner. After eating, Uncle Bernie returned to his bottles, but Kate and her mother settled in front of the television. Kate was permanently disgusted with the reception here. Some of her favorite programs looked as if they were being transmitted from the moon. And tonight, the usual grainy texture was superimposed with faint wiggly lights. It was a rerun, anyway. Tired, she decided to go to bed.

Walking up the dark, narrow stairway, she clutched onto the banister. She could still see the spirally patterns of light. It couldn't have been the TV then, must still be the afterimage of that flash of light in the street. That, plus all the sun and glare of her afternoon's exploring. Maybe she *should* take to wearing dark glasses. She'd hate to give in to her mother's nagging about it, but maybe it could make her look sort of interesting and mysterious.

Kate flipped on her light. Like the rest of the house, her room was odd. Somehow it gave her the feeling of living in a snug, slightly modernized cave. At its front, two tall, narrow windows stretched nearly from floor to ceiling. Outside, under the tangle of climbing yellow roses, green wooden shutters were hooked back to the wall. A few feet in from the windows, the ceiling began sloping down, where a later addition to the house had been built right into the hillside.

Walking to the back wall, she stooped under the low ceiling and pulled open a desk drawer. She'd keep the stone in there. Startled, she looked at her hand. It was empty. All the while walking up the stairs, she'd felt that stone in her hand—and she hadn't thought a thing of it. Really weird.

The thought drifted away as she looked into the drawer. That's where she kept the letters: the ones from those fast friends who'd forgotten her and the ones from her father. His last letter lay on top. She didn't need to read it. She knew it by heart, closing with his usual "Take care of yourself, honey. The world needs you."

Sadness welled up, and she beat it down with resentment. That's what had killed him, thinking that the world and people needed him. She shoved the drawer closed and strode across the room to her bureau. Loosing her straight brown hair, she began brushing at it furiously. He'd always wanted to talk to people, to get to know them, to help them. So whenever a bunch of generals and politicians decided that someone needed our help, that was fine with him.

Kate put down the brush, her blue eyes gazing blankly at the mirror. Well, she wasn't going to be like that. She would not get tied up with people. If they had problems, they could just handle them themselves. Friendships, caring about people—that was only asking for pain.

Her eyes blurred with tears. But suddenly she blinked, focusing them. What was that in the mirror?

Someone was standing behind her, way behind her, as if the back of the room wasn't there. Long gray hair and dark, leathery skin. He was smiling sadly. At her?

Kate spun around. There was no one there. He'd been right there beside the desk. Only the desk hadn't been there, nor had the walls. Just hillside.

She shivered as if the cool night wind were blowing right through the walls. There was absolutely no one with her in the room, not even any suggestive shadows or hanging clothing. She couldn't have seen a thing. Hurriedly, she undressed and dove into bed.

There was no way she could get to sleep, not if she thought about it. So she tried to blank out her mind. And she was tired. Slowly she began feeling warm and comfortable. The smooth, cool weight in her hand was soothing, comforting.

Her eyes snapped open. She clenched her fist. No stone. Deliberately she spread her hand flat and slid it under the pillow to keep it that way. There were no spooky old men, no smooth cool stones. She would go to sleep!

THREE

IN THE MORNING, KATE STILL FELT TENSE AND jumpy. But the next few days seemed relatively normal. At least she saw no visionary people, though occasionally she did feel the weight of a stone in her pocket, or its smooth surface cupped in her hand.

The eye problem, however, did not get better. Instead of gradually fading away, the squiggly lines were becoming clearer. They'd resolved themselves into a pattern: a circle with uneven spokes on the outside and a glowing spiral sinking toward the middle. She didn't see it all the time, only unexpectedly when she was thinking of something else.

Definitely, however, she was not going to tell her mother about it. That would mean trips to some eye doctor in Carson City or Reno. She'd have to talk to simpering nurses and poking doctors. No way. Surely her eyes would get better after a while.

Her biggest problem had nothing to do with eyesight or odd occurrences. Her mother was talking again about her joining the church youth group, about their wonderful wholesome parties and field trips. Kate shuddered. It was bad enough having to mingle with people during the school year, but to do it "voluntarily" during the summer was just too much. There she'd be, sitting by herself during endless futile gatherings, with nothing to say and no one she wanted to say it to. Absolutely no way.

Finally she decided she needed a counteroffer and guessed she'd have to revive Uncle Bernie's get-to-know-the-land scheme. But she wasn't too keen on just wandering out into that dried-up landscape again and watching for snakes. She needed some sort of goal.

That business with the stone was creepy, but it did give her an idea: Indians, the old ones who had lived here long ago. Though how they'd managed to eke out any living in this desert was beyond her. But they were good and dead, so it wouldn't be like getting involved with live people. And they had lived close to the land, miserable as it was, and had known about it. So if she learned about them and, through them, about the land, then maybe her mom and Uncle Bernie would consider that adjustment enough and leave her alone for a while.

One morning, Kate decided to broach the subject to Uncle Bernie while he was weeding. Kate thought that could hardly be much of a task since it ought to be hard enough to get anything to grow here in the first place. But as she approached, he was perched on a stone wall meticulously examining a flower bed and occasionally plucking out errant bits of green.

"Uncle Bernie," she said, sitting on the low wall beside him, "I've decided I'd like to get to know more about Indians. The ones who lived here a long time ago, who lived off the land. You know everything about everything. Tell me something about them."

He laughed with an explosive gust that scattered his neat pile of weeds.

"Ha! Everything about everything! When it comes to things historical, my speciality's the mining days. I can wax eloquent for hours about placer mining, claim jumping, or infamous dance-hall girls. But Indians, now, that's not my field. There's a kid in town, though, who's got a pretty good Indian collection, and then of course, there's your mom's museum. You might start by looking at the Indian stuff there."

Kate thought about the boxes of dusty stones and the arrowheads displayed in geometric patterns on velvet boards. She didn't know what she could learn from those sorts of things.

"Actually, Uncle Bernie, I was thinking more about places where Indians lived. I mean, you said I should get to know the land better, and the Indians knew the land pretty well, didn't they?"

By now her uncle was forced to turn his attention from weeds to his large yellow cat, Scorpio, butting its head vigorously against his weeding arm.

"Oh, I should say they did. To them, every part of nature was inhabited by its own spirit. And in an environment as harsh as this, you'd be courting death if you offended the spirits. Your old Indians wouldn't be dumping toxic wastes in the streams or smog-ifying the air. Scorpio! Finger chewing is no way to express love."

Kate reached out and rubbed the cat behind its battle-scarred ears. "Is there anyplace around here where they lived? You mentioned Indian Cliffs the other night."

"Oh, sure, there're lots of old campsites around. Not much to see, though. They didn't have permanent houses, not like the Pueblo Indians. Life was pretty basic out here, probably more so than any other place in the country. Except for seasonal hunts, they lived in small groups and had to move around after game or pinyon nuts or whatever was ripe. If people couldn't keep up or caused trouble, they were out. No group could afford extra people any more than they could carry around extra material things. Indian Cliffs, though, that's a bit better for seeing something. It's a petroglyph site. The Indians did a bunch of drawings on the rocks. No one today knows what they mean, but they're worth taking a squint at."

A small black butterfly darted by, and Scorpio bounded after it into a bed of sky blue flowers. Kate watched his backward curving tail move through the blossoms like a periscope.

"Sounds pretty good. How do I get there?"

"Easiest way's to follow the gully that starts behind the bank building. Keep to that, past the old mine tailings right on up to the top. You can't miss the Cliffs as long as you stay in that gully and keep going up. At the top there's a sort of low saddle. It's another pass through the peaks, not as low as the one the highway folks chose, but the migratory deer still use it. It's a pretty long hike, though. You might want to take your sleeping bag and spend the night."

21

This last suggestion sounded dreadfully daring and exciting to Kate, but at dinner her mother was less enthusiastic.

"I don't know, Bernie," she said, while serving mashed potatoes. "It doesn't seem right to let a young girl go off camping by herself."

"My dear niece, this is the West, not your decadent, urban East. We don't have muggers behind every boulder. And Indian Cliffs isn't marked in the guides as a tourist attraction—it's too far off the roads. So there won't even be any *traveling* Eastern muggers."

"Well, what about snakes?"

Kate stiffened slightly and concentrated on pouring a perfect lake of gravy into her potatoes.

"Shouldn't be any problem as long as she wears good boots. Besides, it's higher up there, pretty much out of their range. Even around here we're on the borderline."

Great, Kate thought. So she only needed to worry about hardy frontier snakes.

"Besides," Bernie persisted, "if Kate's going to make this place her home, she's got to know it."

"Yes, but the church group . . ."

"The church group is all very well, but a person can't feel at home in a place until they feel comfortable with the land. Getting comfortable with people can come later."

Kate breached the mashed-potato dam, feeling immensely grateful to Uncle Bernie as she watched the freed gravy flood the town of green peas. After a few more faltering objections, her mother gave in. The expedition was on.

VISION QUEST

Three days later, as Kate trudged down the street in her hiking boots, she was less sure that this was a marvelous idea. It was still morning, but already the early coolness had melted into the shadows, and heat was beginning to build. She'd tried to keep her pack light, with mostly food and a down sleeping bag and no cooking equipment. But she hadn't been camping since going with her father, and the straps on her shoulders chaffed and pulled.

She tried not to think about her father and their camping trips, but every thump of her boots or clank of the canteen at her belt reminded her. They'd always gone somewhere green and refreshing: streams and meadows, big cool lakes. With despair, she looked at the weed-filled gully behind the bank. The hillside above was blazened not with waterfalls but with the weatherworn *A* that the kids of Argentum High had painted on the rocks. Smudging back tears, she started climbing.

Around her, rusty cans and old car bodies gradually gave way to rocks, sage, and tufts of yellow-green grass. In the clean, dry air, the sun was so bright that even the plainest pebble sparkled like gold. She kept a wary eye out for snakes, but saw only a few scuttling lizards, their leathery backs set with tiny, sun-catching scales.

Now and again, she also saw the light pattern. Her gaze would idly sweep a blank rock, and there it would be; or its spirals and spokes would suddenly appear in a pattern of pine branches against the sky. She had deliberately worn dark glasses, but they didn't seem to help. The image was clearly coming from inside, not out. Could you permanently sunburn your eyes? The

23

idea wasn't pleasant, but somehow it was better than the other haunting thought that she couldn't quite put into words.

The climb and the heat seemed endless, but at last she dropped into the shade of a juniper to eat some lunch. Munching on jerky and dried apricots, she looked around, trying to imagine the cool greenery of other hikes. But somehow, no other world now seemed possible. In the shimmering midday heat, only the present existed, only this harsh, dry world could ever be real. Real as the ancient tree at her back, real as the cool, smooth stone in her hand.

Quickly Kate opened her hand. She saw nothing. But she had felt it. It had been there. No! Splaying her fingers, she scraped her palm over the rough, twisted bark of the juniper. Then deliberately she stood up, chugged a mouthful of metallic-tasting water from her canteen, and reshouldered her pack. It was just the heat. People weren't meant to walk around in this sort of heat.

But she had a goal. Trying to think only of that, she trudged on up the gully. It was getting narrower, with low, rocky cliffs rising on either side like ancient battlements. No, more like the scenes in all those Westerns, the place for the ambush or maybe where the mountain lion stands majestically against the sky. She wondered if mountain lions had the same aversion to altitude as snakes apparently did. Somehow their name didn't imply it.

The gully broadened slightly where a second dry watercourse cut steeply into it. The sun had baked the world into silence. There was no noise anywhere except for the scrape of her boots and the clatter of pebbles on the slope. Pebbles?

Alarmed, she looked to her left. Something moved, a shadow behind a rock. Slowly she began stepping backward, her eyes never leaving that rock. The air was breathless, hot, and absolutely still.

A voice cut the silence. "Oh, hello. Thought I heard some sort of animal coming."

A person stepped out from behind the rock. "Should have known, though. Only crazy people like me climb around in the middle of the day. What're you doing up here, anyway?"

Kate was so relieved, she forgot to be shy. "Hiking. I can, can't I?"

"Sure." The boy was clambering toward her down the pebbly slope. She recognized him: Jimmy Fong, whose parents ran Argentum's only decent restaurant. "Don't think it's anybody's land in particular. You heading up to Indian Cliffs?"

Still shaky from her scare, Kate nodded, leaning back against a cool, shadowed boulder.

"It's nice up there," Jimmy said. "You just hiking or looking for petroglyphs?"

"Indian things. I want to see Indian places, you know, get an idea of how they lived."

Jimmy sat on a rock, fanning himself with a spiral-bound notebook. "Not much to see of where they lived. They camped there to hunt and pick nuts but didn't leave much behind. The petroglyphs are great, though."

25

"Oh." Kate couldn't think of anything to say. She didn't want to be talking with this kid at all. But it would be rude just to walk away. "What . . . what are you doing up here?"

"I'm after Indian stuff, too. But I'm collecting. I found this spot months ago but haven't been able to really work it. Come on, I'll show you."

He jumped up and began climbing back the way he had come. Kate started to protest, but he was already way ahead. Annoyed, she followed. Sand and smooth stones floored the gully, showing that it sometimes served as a stream.

"This isn't the easiest route, I guess," her guide called back, "but it's the quickest. We cut off here."

He scrambled up the steep bank, sending down a shower of dirt and pebbles. Kate waited for this to settle, then started up herself, creating her own little avalanche. She almost wished that it *had* been a mountain lion. At least it wouldn't have talked to her and insisted on showing her things.

She caught up to Jimmy at a spot where the ground was almost level, a shelf on the edge of a ridge. Dropping away below them was a dry, sage-dotted slope. At one end, sun glinted off the windows of Argentum. Beyond, through a V-shaped gap in the mountains, she glimpsed a broad, gray-green valley and the snow-topped mountains that formed its far wall. A breeze, hot but welcome, ruffled her hair.

"Wonderful, isn't it?" Jimmy said enthusiastically. "Indians could sit here and watch for game. And while they waited, they made tools. Look at all the chips lying around. Flint, mostly, but see, there's a patch of obsidian flakes. Look like broken glass, don't they? I've collected quite a lot already." Proudly he pointed to a neat pile of small matchboxes.

Kate stared, then looked up. "Why, you're a pothunter!"

He frowned. "I am not! I'm an archaeologist."

"You? You're a kid, you can't be. You're just a curio collector, a pothunter."

Jimmy straightened his narrow shoulders. "I am an archaeologist! An amateur now, but I'll be an eminent scholar someday, a recognized authority on Great Basin Indians. For crying out loud, I don't just collect stuff, I record it!"

He waved his notebook in her face. "See, I record everything. I've got this whole site divided into sections, and I sketch every piece in place. Then I put them all in these boxes, every one numbered. See, I'm scientific, systematic!"

"Oh . . . yes . . . I guess so," Kate muttered, trying to figure out how to get out of this. "It's pretty important, I guess, so maybe I shouldn't take up any more of your time. Can I get to Indian Cliffs if I just head up along this ridge?"

Jimmy looked a little disappointed but shook his head. "No, that'd take you too far north. Better go back and continue the way you were going."

"Okay, thanks. See you around." Almost as if a mountain lion were really after her, Kate scurried back down to the larger gully.

Starting up it again, she muttered to herself about too

friendly people. It had probably been rude to run off like that, but she wished some people wouldn't be so chummy and insist on dragging other people into their lives. If she'd stuck around, he'd probably have been nauseatingly helpful and escorted her to the cliffs.

And help she didn't need. She couldn't really get lost now. The gully was becoming steeper and narrower. Each side was set with boulders, and between them grew scrubby pinyon pine and darker gnarled juniper.

Quite suddenly, the gully opened out. She'd come at last to the pass, a sloping saddle between two peaks. Pale red cliffs and boulders edged both sides. The area was huge. It would be impossible to find a few rock drawings among all this.

She walked forward, her boots crunching on the gravelly earth. It was cooler up here, but without the sound of her boots there'd be utter silence. No bird calls, no insect chirpings, nothing. Back East, the wilderness was full of noises: whistles and chirps and things scurrying in the dense green growth. But here, life was thin, dry, and silent.

It didn't make her feel lonely, though, just alone. Maybe the West wasn't all that bad, she decided suddenly. At least, if you worked at it, you could be alone here.

Walking slowly toward the eastern cliffs, Kate studied their scuffed rock walls. Suddenly she realized those scars weren't as random and natural as she'd thought. The Indian drawings! Excited, she slipped off her pack and scrambled up the lower slopes.

On the reddish stone, the pale, scraped designs

showed like old scars. Crisscrosses, circles alone or linked together, ladder marks, wavy lines, arches. Here and there were shapes that might be animals, things with legs or horns. And there were a few that could have been people.

For a couple of hours, she climbed along the eastern cliff and then on the lower one across from it. There'd be patches of unmarked rock, then she'd come across another cluster of drawings. It was as exciting as hunting treasure.

What had they meant? Had they been some sort of alphabet? Did maybe a wavy line mean *A* and an oval mean *B*? Or was it sort of picture writing? Did one cluster mean "I walked to the mountain, it rained, I turned right and saw three deer"? She wondered if anyone knew. "Eminent" scholars like Jimmy Fong, maybe? Ha!

Finally she realized it was getting hard to tell the drawings from natural cracks in the rock. She looked around her. Dusk filled the mountain pass like smoke. She'd better choose a place to camp and eat some dinner.

After a short search, she found a shallow depression at the base of the western cliff. It was about the right size for a sleeping bag and looked free of jabby stones. She fetched her pack and began rummaging around for food.

Switching on her flashlight to see into the pack, she suddenly realized that she had not seen the spirally lights for some time. Then maybe they *were* just some sort of light burn. They had to be, really—no other explanation. Uneasily she turned her attention back to dinner.

The tuna, crackers, apple, and granola bar left her content. Sitting on the unrolled sleeping bag, she leaned back against a large rock and watched the sky. Slowly it turned from smoky pink to violet, through deeper and deeper shades of purple. A few jewellike stars were joined by more and more until the sky glittered with them.

Now the area around her awakened a little. A pair of birds called back and forth from opposite cliffs; scattered insects chattered dryly; and a high, thin wind seemed to blow down from the stars. It sighed brittlely among the trees and loosed a clean, sharp smell of sage and pine.

Kate wanted to stay awake. Here, away from city lights, she could watch the multiplying stars and maybe even see some falling ones. But the day had been tiring, and the rock behind her was rough and cold.

Sleepily she turned her head to look at the rock, then played her flashlight over its surface. She'd seen the petroglyphs higher up but hadn't noticed this one right beside her. Or was it one? She ran her fingers through three curved grooves. Yes, someone had sat here once and made them. Who and why? Shrugging sleepily, she snuggled down into her bag. In the distance, she heard the high wail of a coyote. Even that didn't sound lonely. It belonged.

For an hour Kate slept dreamlessly while night things went about their flitting, scurrying business, unconcerned by her small intrusion. Then she woke with a sharp, jabbing pain in her back. Must have been a rock under her after all. She shifted uncomfortably and tried to sink back into sleep.

But now her attention was caught by something else: a pinpoint of light on the top of the eastern cliff. Someone with a flashlight? A camp fire? Then she noticed that the sky around it was glowing, the stars almost blotted out. And the chink of light was growing.

Alarmed, she sat up. Then she laughed aloud, breaking the waiting stillness. The moon was rising behind trees on the mountain crest.

Slowly the moon became fuller, impossibly large, impossibly bright. Like smoke, a misty light flowed through the valley, transforming the sage, pine, and juniper. Dark, shapeless night forms changed into feathery phantoms of their daytime selves. Finally, the moon cleared the mountain rim, a full, blinding white circle. The smudgy marks on its surface were comfortingly familiar.

As Kate watched, mesmerized by the brightness, those marks seemed to change shape. Within the circle of the moon, a spiral began to form. Jutting spokes of light fringed the disk, and the spiral began turning inward, pulling her with it.

She threw herself back against the boulder, fighting to tear away. But the glowing spiral pulled at her, pulled her into deep, ancient visions.

FOUR

FROM HIS FAVORITE SITTING ROCK, WADAT looked out over the high little valley, the rock-walled pass through the mountains. At one end of the pass, misty coils of blue smoke rose into the air, carrying the familiar pungent smell of burning sage.

His mother would be down there with the other women winnowing and roasting this year's harvest of pine seed. From his perch, Wadat could see them now, moving among the huts of bent branches and sage brush. Laughter rose up like birdcalls. They had reason for happiness. The pines had been generous this year. With their seeds his people should survive another winter.

Of course, it was the hunt that would make that certain. With greater interest, Wadat shifted his position on the sun-warmed rock and looked to the other end of the pass. As busy as ants, the men and boys were building the fences of sagebrush that would channel the migrating deer, that would send them right under the cliffs where the skilled archers would be waiting, silent and patient as the rock.

VISION QUEST

Basking in the sun, he thought of other hunts and the part he could play in this one. But something else kept pricking at his attention. For minutes now, he had felt something watching him.

Up here, there was hardly anywhere for even a lizard to hide. Yet something was watching. A spirit perhaps? He was training to be a shaman, so it wasn't surprising that he should feel a spirit's presence. Often one could sense them in the quiet sleeping rock, in the night whispers of pine, or in the soaring of a hawk on the wind's high pathways. But somehow this felt different.

His people had behaved rightly to the spirits of this place. When they had arrived this year, they had sung the prayers and songs for greeting the mountains and the trees, and for asking them to share the seeds that would let his people live another season. Still, a curious or suspicious spirit might drop by to see that the people were not being greedy or doing the land any harm.

Well, spirits could come and go about their land as they chose. Wadat whispered ritual words of spirit-greeting, then turned his attention back to the fence building. He'd like to be down there helping with the other boys. But Hizu, the shaman, had asked that he come to him. Already he'd put it off too long, sitting on this rock and dreaming.

Sighing, Wadat stood up and began climbing along the cliff. Hizu had a cave up here where he could consult with the spirits and, Wadat knew, take untroubled naps. But he wouldn't make fun of the old man. Hizu was a powerful shaman, but more, he was Wadat's special friend.

VISION QUEST

When families went their separate ways after the hunts, the shaman and his family, if he had one, would choose to travel with one group or another. Hizu was an old man now and alone, and in recent years he had often chosen to join Wadat's family. He had treated Wadat as a son and taught him the ways of a shaman.

Wadat stopped outside of Hizu's cave. The strange spirit was still with him, but it didn't feel malevolent, just—lonely? Could a spirit be lonely among so many? Shrugging, Wadat stepped into the cool dim cave.

Hizu was bent forward, his long gray hair almost sweeping the dust. But he wasn't napping. Wadat could see him tracing a pattern onto the floor of the cave.

The old man looked up, a smile adding another set of creases to his lined leathery face. Nodding wordlessly, he pointed to the rock where Wadat usually sat. On it lay a deerskin pouch. It looked like a shaman's medicine pouch, only it was new, not worn and stained like Hizu's. Gingerly the boy picked it up, then looked questioningly at the shaman.

"Wadat, it is time for you to begin collecting your own medicine things. Things that have meaning for you, that have power for you, that spirits show you in dreams."

Wadat felt the soft bag. A heavy lump lay at one end of it. "There's something there already."

"The gift of an old shaman to a new one. The pattern for it came to me in a dream. I don't know the meaning of it, but perhaps in time the spirits will show you."

Wadat slid his hand into the bag and pulled out a cool, smooth stone. He turned it over in his hand. It was

34

formed into a tapering cylinder, and its deep red surface was marked with three curving grooves.

Wadat looked up in awe. "A charm stone."

"You will need it when you set out to seek your guardian spirit. And that time must come soon, Wadat."

The boy swallowed uncomfortably and looked down at the stone in his hand. The vision quest. Surely he wasn't ready for that yet? He tried to keep his voice steady. "This stone is a lot like yours, Hizu."

The old man nodded and reached for the worn pouch at his own side. "Perhaps because we have been so close. The spirit showed me the shape and color yours was to be. It is like mine, yet different." He reached into his bag, felt for a moment, and pulled out another stone cylinder.

Wadat squatted down and watched closely. Seldom had Hizu shown him the contents of his medicine bag. They were powerful magic and very personal. Now Hizu's own charm stone lay on his withered palm. Smooth and black, a single groove spiraling from one tapered end to the other.

Gently he placed it on the ground, and Wadat put his own stone beside it. They seemed like twins except that one was black and one red, one was carved with a spiraling groove and the other with three curved lines.

Wadat reached toward them, then stopped. He felt another reaching as well. Hizu seemed to sense it, too, and stared at the cave entrance. Quickly, Wadat looked around.

He saw it now, the strange spirit. Its faint shimmering image stood at the mouth of the cave. It had taken the form of a human girl. A girl with moon-pale skin and wide frightened eyes.

He met those eyes, and the presence vanished.

Kate's eyes flew open, then jammed closed again. Bright light had burned into them. Her heart was still racing fearfully from the dream. It had been a dream. It had!

Cautiously she opened her eyes again. The light was the sun, newly risen over the eastern cliff. Already it was warming the air, making her sleeping bag almost too snug.

She unzipped it but still did not sit up. What a susceptible ninny she'd been! She'd talked with that Jimmy Fong character, looked at some old rock drawings, and pretty soon she was having weird dreams about Indians. She'd even understood them when they talked, though the old-time Indians, if that was what they were supposed to be, surely wouldn't have spoken English.

Her subconscious had really worked overtime putting stuff together. There was this valley, the stone Pete the pothunter had left, and even the old gray-haired man her imagination had conjured up a few days earlier. She shivered. Dreadful dreams. Not that anything really dreadful had happened. But it had all been so dreadfully real, as if she had been right there, a lost spirit watching a fragment of some ancient boy's real life.

She rolled over and felt a jab in her side. That blasted pointy rock again. Sitting up, she felt angrily around the shallow hollow. A sharp rock protruded from the dirt.

Scrabbling at it with her fingers, she wiggled and tugged until it suddenly popped out like a loose tooth. It was about three inches long, a smooth cylinder with two tapered ends.

Kate dropped it like a snake, and stared at it lying in the dust. Its dark red surface was marked with three curved grooves. Wadat's stone.

Angrily she shook her head. That was crazy. Her mind had just dreamed up that person. But the stone itself was real, a real Indian artifact. And sort of pretty, too. Cautiously she picked it up, enjoying the smooth cool weight in her hand. It felt right, sort of comforting. An hour later, when she had dressed, breakfasted, and reshouldered her pack, the stone was riding in her jeans pocket, a cool smooth weight—and a real one.

Three days later, Kate was much less happy with her find. At night she kept it in the drawer with her father's letters, but during the day she carried it around in the pocket of her jeans or jacket. Not that she wanted to, but whenever she tried to leave it behind, she felt so anxious about it, she had to rush back and stuff it into her pocket.

The problem was, it often wasn't alone. Sometimes she'd feel a weight in the other pocket, too, and when she'd reach in, she'd seem to touch something, another shape just as cool and smooth. But when she really groped around and turned her pocket out, there'd be nothing there. Only one pocket held a real stone.

What's more, the lights had come back, too, the spoked spiral of light. She'd see it when and where she least expected it: in the drain of the bathroom sink, on a fried egg at breakfast, in the fur patterns on Scorpio the cat. After what had happened, or seemed to have happened, it was harder to pretend that this thing was just some minor eye problem or that it had nothing to do with Indians or old stones.

And as she thought about it one afternoon, sprawled out on the living-room couch, she realized that all this really did revolve around the stones. None of this had bothered her before she'd picked up that stone the pothunter had left. And then she'd slept on another stone, taken it home, carried it around. That had been stupid. She should get rid of the real stone. After that everything would surely be all right.

Jumping up, she flew out the door, yelling into the house that she was going for a walk. She should have done this days ago. Get rid of the stone and get rid of the problem.

Not far down the road was a dry eroded gully. For years it had been used as a town dump, and now it sported everything from old cars and refrigerators to rusty tin cans and plastic jugs. Weeds grew vigorously amid the junk. Wildflowers peeked out of coiled bedsprings, and sage burst boldly through shattered door frames. The perfect place for something unwanted.

Not allowing herself a moment's thought, she reached into her pocket, pulled out the stone, and with all her strength hurled it into the dump.

Satisfied, she lowered her hand—and found the stone still there. She hadn't thrown it at all!

Gasping, she tried again, forcing her fingers to open.

This time she saw the stone leave her hand and arch through the air. It hit with a clatter among a pile of old cans, then slithered out of sight. She looked down. Her hand was truly empty.

Then, like a blow it hit her, a staggering wave of loss. Old, deep loss. They were moving again, another best friend had forgotten her, her father was dead; and under all this were other losses, deeper, older.

Whimpering like a hurt animal, she scrambled down into the gully, clattering through cans and cartons until she came to the spot where the stone had disappeared. Frantically she pawed about, trying not to cut herself but getting more panicky by the moment. Then she saw it, a smooth, blood red stone, sitting quietly under the blade of an old window fan.

Prying it free, Kate dropped it into her pocket. Calm washed over her like a wave of cool water. Slowly she climbed up out of the dump. At the gully's edge lay a single tin can. With a despairing kick she sent it bouncing and clanging down the rutty road. No good, no good at all! What was she going to do?

Stalking up the road, she kicked whatever came her way: rocks, pinecones, a dog-chewed bone. Well, the first thing she had to do was stop being angry and think systematically. That's what her dad would have said.

She slowed to a thoughtful walk. Okay, she thought. Point one: these Indian stones are really doing weird things to me. Point two: if I want to keep from going bananas, I've got to get rid of this one. Point three: I can't get rid of it without going even more bananas. Point four: so I've got to figure out something else.

She stopped dead. Which led her where? She frowned in thought, oblivious to the scruffy dog that trotted down the road and snuffled at her before going on its way. She had to find out more about the stones. If she knew what they were, then maybe she could figure why they were doing this—and stop them. Which led to what? The museum collection was jumbled and useless. Uncle Bernie said he knew nothing about Indians, but there was one person in town who did.

Her stomach tightened. There was no way she was going to talk to that chummy know-it-all pothunter, Jimmy Fong. No way.

At ten the next morning, Kate stood nervously outside the Silver Palace, the Fongs' Chinese-American restaurant. She'd do anything rather than spend another night like the one she'd just had.

It had started well enough. The lights had bothered her only a little while playing Parcheesi with Uncle Bernie; the need to outdo his wily, little green markers kept her mind off weird things. Then she'd gone to bed and fallen asleep with no trouble.

But in the night, the wind wakened her. It blew through the cottonwoods, whistling and sighing; it blew with a soft haunting tune. From her bed, Kate could see the seed fluff from the cottonwoods blowing past her window, looking in the moonlight like down fallen from angel wings.

She got out of bed and padded across the cold floorboards to the window. The moonlit garden was lovely. Every flower and shrub had a new pale color. Before she knew it, she had pulled on a jacket, slipped the stone into a pocket, and started quietly downstairs. It was all so beautiful, she needed a better look.

It was breathtakingly beautiful, and the high tune in the cottonwoods blew on and on. The moon-washed garden looked like a place she'd never seen before. And then suddenly she realized she hadn't, not like this.

It was as if two photographs had been taken at the same time. The misty picture of her uncle's garden was overlaid by another. In the second picture, the hillside was uncut, unterraced, unplanted. It grew wild with sage and pine. On that slope, two figures walked, an old man and a boy. There the air was filled with music, not from the wind but from a bone pipe the man played as he walked.

The two misty figures stopped. Kate could see them over by the stone bench, only the bench was hardly there. Mostly, there was a low bush with spiky yellow leaves. Slowly she walked toward them.

The old man stopped playing the flute and squatted down beside the bush, gesturing for the boy to join him. "This is how you must seek it. If you pull up these roots in the sunlight or without asking permission of the plant and the earth, then they will be worthless, even poisonous. But if you wait until the moon is full and play the proper tune for the spirits, asking their aid, then the roots will be full of power. They will drive off headache and fever."

He grabbed up a stick and began poking gently at the ground. "Now, you play the tune while I dig. Can you remember it?"

Wadat nodded. He reached into the leather pouch at

41

his side and pulled out his own flute. The slender white bone glowed in the moonlight. Slowly he began to play.

The tune was the same, the high clear tune that Kate had heard in the trees, the tune that had called her out. And it called still. She stepped closer to the pair while the hillside around them became more and more solid. Under it, the garden faded to a phantom shadow.

The tune faltered and stopped. With wide surprised eyes, the boy looked into her own. Tentatively, he reached out a hand.

"No!" Crying out like a night bird, Kate fled back into the garden.

FIVE

STANDING IN THE WARM MORNING SUN, KATE STILL shivered at the memory. Not that it had really been all that frightening. There'd been no nightmare monsters, after all. But *that's* what was so frightening. It hadn't been a nightmare. She hadn't been asleep. This morning she'd awakened on top of her bed, still wearing her jacket and covered with dirt and scratches. From her window, she could see where she had walked right through a rosebush while she'd been seeing only a wild hillside and a boy and a man gathering medicine roots.

Still, only a short passage of time had made last night seem less dreadful than the prospect before her. Her stomach tightened, and she felt clammy and ill. She'd have to go in there, talk to who knows how many people, and then tell Jimmy Fong that she needed his help. She wanted to turn and run.

Instead she walked like a condemned criminal across the street to the Silver Palace. The sagging second-story balcony jutting like a canopy over the plank sidewalk created a shaded sanctuary. Kate hardly noticed it as she stared apprehensively through the open door on the saloon side of the building.

It was dim inside. The crystal chandeliers were unlit at this hour, and the only light seemed to come from the winking and flashing of a slot machine, which a customer was steadily feeding coins. The sound was hypnotic. The clank of the handle, the whirring and jangling. Silence, another coin, another clank of the handle.

Kate looked away. Along one wall, a carved mahogany bar stretched into the gloom. Behind it, the long mirror reflected two customers seated on stools and someone in a white apron fussing with bottles. Mr. Fong, maybe. She did not want to go in there.

Quickly she walked to the second door. The restaurant inside was even less busy but decidedly cheerier. Sunlight streamed in through tall side windows, lighting the walls with their fans and scrolls of painted goldfish. Exotic-looking lanterns hung from the high ceiling, trailing silky red tassels.

This was Argentum's only real restaurant, besides an amazingly greasy pizza place, and Kate had liked the times they'd eaten here. She and her mom usually ordered sweet-and-sour pork while Uncle Bernie stuck to the American dishes.

Now she stepped hesitantly inside. Only two people seemed to be there. A very little girl sat in a sunny patch on the floor putting together a large picture puzzle of Big Bird. Nearby, Mrs. Fong moved quickly about setting tables for lunch, whisking silverware, glasses, and paper-packaged chopsticks from a cart beside her.

Kate walked forward, wishing she were invisible. "Uh . . . excuse me, Mrs. Fong. Is Jimmy here?"

The woman looked up and smiled briefly. "Yes, yes. He's in the kitchen, or should be. That way."

Gratefully Kate hurried in the direction indicated, only to face another ordeal at the swinging kitchen doors. Well, she had to go through with it now. She peeped through one of the little round windows, then cautiously pushed a door open.

Inside, the air was steamy and filled with the clatter of dishes. At a table, an older girl was vigorously chopping vegetables with a mean-looking cleaver. A boy stood by a double sink, arms elbow-deep in suds.

The sister looked up but said nothing as Kate walked slowly toward the sink. "Jimmy?"

He turned and looked at her. "Oh, it's you."

Silence. "Yes . . . I . . . I just wanted to apologize for calling you a pothunter."

"Oh, that's okay, I guess." He grinned as he pushed straight black hair out of his eyes, leaving a smear of suds. "See, I'm really just a pot washer."

She felt a little better. "Yeah, that's right. Well, I found something up at Indian Cliffs I thought you might like to see, since you're interested in Indian stuff and all."

"Really?" He looked quickly across the room. "Let's go out on the porch away from bossy big sisters."

Wiping his hands on an apron, Jimmy led the way to a side door. The little porch looked out over a rubble-filled lot.

"I've never found much of anything at Indian Cliffs," Jimmy said leaning against the railing. "Just a few stone chips and fire-burned rocks. What've you got?"

Slowly Kate reached into her pocket and pulled the

stone into the sunlight. Lying cool in her palm, it glowed a deep blood red.

Jimmy's breath whistled in. "Wow. That's really something. A charm stone. I've sure never found anything like that. Where was it?"

"Half buried below one of the petroglyph rocks. It kept jabbing my back while I was sleeping." She had no intention of mentioning the dream.

"What luck!"

"You called it a charm stone. Could you . . . uh . . . could you tell me what that is?"

"That's what archaeologists call stones like that, ones ground into smooth shapes. Sometimes they have patterns or are shaped like animal heads or something. No one really knows what they were used for."

Kate kept looking at him expectantly.

"I mean, they don't seem to be tools or jewelry or anything. When they're found, they're usually with the sort of things a shaman might have, so some people think they might have been used for magic. Maybe shamans cast charms with them or saw visions or something. No one knows really."

"Oh, well, I guess that's something." This was hardly the sort of information Kate had hoped for, but at least it gave her some idea of what the stone was, if not how to deal with it. "Thanks, I . . ."

"I'll show you my collection upstairs. I've got a couple of broken pieces that might be charm stones, unless they're pendants or weights."

"No, I really should . . ." But Jimmy was already heading back through the kitchen. Frowning, Kate felt forced to follow. He disappeared through a back door and headed up a narrow wooden staircase. Halfway up, they met a younger brother clattering down.

"Oh-oh," the kid said as he squeezed by, "Jimmy's taking a girlfriend to his bedroom!"

"Shut up, jerk!" Jimmy retorted. "She's not a girlfriend, just a professional acquaintance who is a girl."

Blushing as red as a fire truck, Kate wished she could disappear, but Jimmy kept leading her through the back ways of the Silver Palace.

In the old days, the upstairs had been a hotel, but now its rooms were used by the Fongs, with each of the five children having a separate room. Jimmy proudly opened the door to his.

The faded wallpaper was almost hidden under posters and photos, not of rock stars or movies but pages from *National Geographic* and travel posters showing scenes of the Southwest. A bed and bureau took up one corner. The rest of the room was crammed with bookshelves and tables piled with file folders, boxes, maps, and bits of stone. "My study," Jimmy said grandly.

Kate's expression wavered between cynicism and interest. She stepped up to one of the tables and pointed to a pile of black stone chips. "Those are the ones you found in the gully the other day?"

"Right. I'm numbering them by where they came from. Then they get stored on those shelves, and the site records go here. I worked out the system myself."

Kate picked up a small sharp flake that glinted like a bit of broken glass. "You really want to be an archaeologist?"

"I *am* an archaeologist. I want to be an eminent

scholar. I want to get lots of degrees, teach at a big university, and do fieldwork every year."

Kate sighed. At least he knew what he wanted. All she knew was what she *didn't* want. "I bet your parents are disgustingly proud of you."

"Them? They're dead set against it. At least my father is."

"Why? Isn't the money any good?"

"It's not just that; it's the tradition. The Silver Palace. It's a family business, run by the Fongs for generations. My life's all plotted out. Instead of making scholarly breakthroughs at some great university, I'll be making wontons in Nowhere Town, Nevada—forever." He kicked at a chair leg.

"But there are lots of kids in your family. Couldn't someone else run the family business?"

"It was supposed to be my brother George who did it; he's the oldest son. But he put his foot down early, and now he's studying engineering on a college scholarship. Since my dad's lost one, he'll never let me get away."

"Maybe if you show him you're really good at what you do."

"What do you think all this is?" He gestured around the room.

"Yeah. I see."

Jimmy scowled a moment, then sighed. "Well anyway, that's my problem not yours. I'll show you the stones." He pulled out a drawer, sorted through boxes, then gently dumped the contents of one onto the table. There were several smooth stones, obviously manmade and obviously broken. Kate was almost afraid to touch them, but when she did, she felt nothing special.

"They could be charm stones," Jimmy said, "but it's hard to tell. You know if there's anything like them over at the museum?"

"Not me. I don't imagine anyone knows, that stuff's so jumbled. My mom wants to work on it, but it's not first on her list. She's doing the mining stuff now."

"Hmm. How about you doing me a favor?"

"A favor?" Kate tensed. This was just what she was afraid of. Get involved with anybody, even a little bit, and pretty soon there were more and more obligations. "I don't know. . . ."

"Hey, come on. I told you about charm stones."

"I just brought mine so you could see it."

"Don't give me that. You wanted to know what you had, and I told you." He frowned impatiently. "Well then, don't think of it as a favor. Think of it as a consulting fee. A purely business arrangement."

"Well . . ."

"As trade for my information, I want you to ask your mom if I can come to the museum and look through all their unsorted Indian stuff. Museums do that all the time. Visiting scholars studying the collection. Lets say, two o'clock tomorrow afternoon."

Kate seethed. She'd really walked into this one. Still, if she did it, then any obligation would be cancelled. Like he said, a one-for-one business arrangement.

"Oh, all right. I'll ask my mother and let you know. But that's it."

"A deal. It's been a pleasure doing business with you."

Kate grumbled to herself all the way home. Some

business deal. Well, at least if she kept things on that footing, no personal favors, then any debt could be disposed of once and for all.

Grimly she brought up the subject at dinner. Mrs. Elliot smiled broadly, cast a knowing glance at Uncle Bernie, and said that it was a lovely idea. She'd be happy to let Kate's friend see the collection.

"He's not my friend!" Kate objected. "Just an acquaintance who knows about Indian things."

"And I've heard he has a very fine collection," her mother replied. "Maybe he can tell us something about ours. Yes, two o'clock will be fine. You two can spend the afternoon there."

"*I'm* not planning to be there!"

"Oh, but you really have to, Kate. I have my regular work to do, and the board wouldn't want me to let someone into the storeroom unsupervised."

"What good would my being there do?"

"Oh, it's really just a formality, but I can't let him do it otherwise."

Mercilessly, Kate mashed the diced carrots with her fork. "Oh, all right. I'll be there." She doubted that the museum board had any such rule. Her mom had probably made it up so she'd be forced to be social with someone. Still, it was better than the church youth group—maybe.

By noon the next day, Kate was in a deep funk, grasping at straws. Maybe he'd forget, maybe his parents wouldn't let him get away. If he didn't show, she decided, that was it. This was a one-time deal.

After lunch she trudged down the hill and helped her

mother rearrange a case of old glass insulators. Promptly at two o'clock, Jimmy Fong walked through the museum's front door. He looked cheerfully around, ignoring Kate's hostile stare. Mrs. Elliot bubbled a greeting, then ushered the two of them into a back storeroom.

Sullenly Kate pointed to a pile of dusty boxes huddled under a table. "My mom says most of the Indian stuff's in those. Just make sure everything gets back in the right box."

"Of course, I will," Jimmy said indignantly, then he set to work like a kid opening Christmas packages.

Kate slouched onto a stool and watched gloomily as Jimmy spread out the contents of box after box, ex claiming and taking notes. She tried to show no interest at all.

This is ridiculous, she thought after a while. Jimmy Fong isn't going to steal any of this stuff, and if he did, who cared? She just had to get away.

Abruptly she jumped off her stool. "I'm going into the next room. Maybe there're some other Indian things stored there."

She closed the door behind her and flipped on the light. Dusty clutter towered on every side. Beside her was an old pump organ with keys missing in it like gaping teeth. Behind it loomed a huge stuffed bear, retired from exhibition after the moths had worked it over. Stacked everywhere were baby carriages, furniture, and mysterious pieces of mining machinery.

Kate walked to the far end of the room. There *were* some Indian things there, but it was also as far from the

51

eminent scholar as she could get. Not that Jimmy was all that bad, she admitted. But she didn't want anything to do with other kids whether they were "all that bad" or not.

Large flat stones crouched along the wall, surfaces pitted by generations of nut cracking. Beside them ranged piles of dust-dulled baskets from more recent Indians. There were also several rough slabs of rock with petroglyphs carved into them.

Kate knelt down by these. One showed nothing but faint crisscrossed lines. An irregular chain of circles connected by lines snaked across another. Casually she traced the pattern with her eyes, then her fingers. Slowly she relaxed and became aware of the stone in her pocket, an odor of sage, and a faint wind-blown melody.

For a moment she fought, trying to keep hold of the silent musty room. But already she could see the hillside, fresh with sun and sage, and the boy who stood beside the carved stone.

Wadat looked at the stone and at the pale fresh cuts where Hizu had recorded his dream. The spirits had shown the shaman what he must do, and he had recorded it on stone, then done what it told him. He had danced first to the east, then turned in a circle, took a few steps, turned twice, then shuffled westward to end in a final turning. And all the while he had chanted the song that the spirits had taught him, the song that asked their permission and their assistance in the hunt.

The hunt that followed had been successful enough,

though not remarkable. The families who had joined in it would have dried meat for at least the coldest months. Yet Wadat had heard grumbling that the old man was losing his power. That frightened him. His people lived so close to the edge, they could afford no mercy for a failing shaman. The only hope was that full stomachs would silence the complaints for a while.

Wadat leaned against the rock to still his trembling. How could anyone question Hizu's power? The shaman walked with the spirits and listened to them; they sang to him and guided him and he knew their ways. Mysterious ways they were and sometimes dangerous. But the spirits would help people if those ways were respected.

Hizu had guided his people for long years. Surely he must continue. Wadat was sure that he himself could never do as well. True, when he was shaded by a tree or rested on a rock he did feel close to those spirits, but never had they spoken to him. They had never guided him or shown him mysteries. Yet still Hizu was confident that he would be the next shaman.

Wadat shook his head despairingly. He enjoyed the teaching and felt that perhaps he could become a minor healer. But never a shaman. He had thought the old man would tire of that idea. But instead he was forcing it to the testing. He had sent Wadat out on the great trial, on his vision quest.

Now he must roam the wilderness, without food or drink, until a spirit found him, possessed him, made him its own. For a great shaman, it must be a powerful spirit like the sun spirit that had chosen Hizu. But would such a one come to him? Wadat doubted it. He could feel the spirit of a basking lizard or a wind spirit wafting by on a whirl of dust. He could even feel that strange lonely spirit that was watching him again, watching and afraid. Yet a powerful spirit, a mountain lion or a bear, what had they to do with him?

Dreamer, he scolded himself. You've gone no farther than the cliffs about the camp. Get up and seek, or even a lizard spirit won't bother with you.

For hours he sought, and then for days. Timeless, the watching spirit trailed behind him, yet he sensed no other. Hunger hurt at first, then became a dull constant ache that drained his strength like an open wound. But it was thirst that caused the torment. His lips cracked, and his tongue swelled, and his skin shriveled and dried like a long-dead lizard's.

Yet still no spirit met him. He took shelter in rocky caves, yet no earth spirit touched him. For hours he watched animals go about their lives, yet none reached out to him with its spirit.

At last, with frenzied desperation, he headed for the mountain peaks. If no spirit found him there, at least he would die in a place of beauty.

With fading strength, he dragged himself upward, toward the highest crags. His whole body throbbed with heat and weakness. Would he never reach the top? Would he fail even here?

Using a last shred of strength, he gripped a stone ledge and painfully pulled himself up and over. He met eyes.

Two round golden eyes stared at him, one from either side of a sharp hooked beak. Startled, young eagle and boy stared at each other, until the beak opened and a harsh cry knifed into the air.

From high above, it was answered. Wadat could not move, could not take his eyes from the dark fierce eaglet. Closer came the answering cry, and then it was upon him, all feathers, noise, and talons.

Three claws, sharp as obsidian, raked his face. His grip loosened, and he fell to darkness on the rocks below.

SIX

A VOICE SPOKE TO WADAT IN THE DARKNESS. IT spoke of the crystal sky, of soaring on warm drafts wafting from the earth, of gliding by mountainous white clouds, and of seeing hills and valleys and streams, all in one timeless glance.

The voice spoke of all the spirits, great and small, that moved beneath its wings or that floated with it through the air or that shone far above it, blazing in the day or glimmering in the cold and distant night.

And the voice sang. It sang songs of many spirits and its own song, songs of power and of beginnings, songs of worlds hidden and mysterious.

The songs went on, endlessly varied and the same, like the wind, like the stars. And a new song blended with them. Not new, old. One heard long ago.

It was Hizu's song, the song the shaman used to call into the spirit world, to bring things forth. Wadat felt a gentle tug. Feebly he resisted. He did not want to leave, to forego all that the eagle spirit was teaching him. But the cradling talons loosed him, and he slid again into the world.

He felt a hand under his head and a water jug at his lips. He sucked at it like a thirsty puppy. The old man's song shifted into quiet, coaxing talk.

"There, you are back. Stay with us now, brave one. A great spirit has made you its own, and you have much to teach us. So you must stay with us, you see."

Through parched throat, Wadat tried to croak out questions. "Where . . . how . . . ?"

"When you had not returned in several days, I set out to find you. If nothing else, I could give your body its proper rites. But when I found you at last beneath the eagle's craig, life still fluttered in you, though your spirit was clearly soaring elsewhere. The eagle watched me as I lifted you. You bore her mark on your cheek, yet helpless as you were, she had done you no further harm. She let me take you back to your own world, though I think her spirit has been with you all this while."

Wadat looked into the old man's eyes and above them at the spiral sun-sign woven into the band at his forehead. Slowly the boy raised a hand to where his cheek burned with dull pain. Wincing, he traced three curved gashes.

The old man nodded his head. "Now we know why the spirit told me to put three curved lines on your charm stone, even as mine has its spiral. When you are recovered, you must choose a great rock and carve that same mark upon it."

Fumbling in the pouch at his side, Wadat pulled out his charm stone. Hizu helped him sit, and their two hands met over the stone. Slowly a third hand joined these. Wadat stared at it, then traced the pale shadow up the arm to shoulder and face. His eyes met the strange, frightened eyes. Then, like a flash of lightning, they were gone.

Jimmy was in his element: boxes and boxes of unlabeled Indian artifacts. Nothing stood between them and oblivion but one lone scholar illuminating their dusty heaps with the light of knowledge.

He rather wished Kate hadn't gone off. He knew she wasn't fond of being with people, and he could think of other kids besides standoffish Kate Elliot he'd rather have with him. But he needed someone with whom to share his great scholarly discoveries.

After awhile, the sheer amount of material began to overwhelm him. He hoped Mrs. Elliot would let him come back often, because it would take ages to go through all this. And Kate had said there was more Indian stuff in the other room. Where was she anyway?

Jimmy stood up and looked around, suddenly realizing he really didn't like being in the room alone. It wasn't the old Indian stuff that bothered him. Somehow it was so old that it seemed clean and dry. It was the more recent stuff that seemed kind of creepy. Like bones with flesh still on them.

Timidly he opened the door to the other room. If anything, it was more dim and musty than the one he had been in, and clearly most of the mounded stuff had nothing to do with Indians. Wheelbarrows full of tools; coatracks and grandfather clocks; a weird headless mannequin wearing a moth-eaten uniform; Victrolas, carriages, molting birds under glass domes.

"Kate?" he whispered.

The dusty silence swallowed his voice. Had it swallowed her, too? Nonsense. She'd probably slipped out a back door to get away from him.

Indignation gave his voice strength. "Kate!"

Nothing. He walked farther into the maze. An old glass-windowed coffin leaned against a wall, inviting him to peer in. He averted his eyes. One definitely should not look into coffins. A wardrobe loomed beside him, large and dark. It's door opened into blackness that smelled of rot and dead things.

"Kate!"

He saw her by the far wall, seated among tombstones. No, they were Indian stones. Relieved and annoyed, he walked toward her. "Kate, why didn't you answer. I was . . ."

She hadn't moved. He looked down at her face. She stared with absolute blankness at one of the stones.

"Kate, Kate Elliot!" He put a hand on her shoulder. Then, with a cry, he reeled back, overcome by a powerful shock and by a brief, strange, and very vivid picture. He shook his head to clear it, then saw Kate doing the same. She gave him a bewildered stare.

"You sure have some static electricity around here," he quavered.

"Jimmy. I'd forgotten. Did you . . . uh . . . did you see?"

"I was wondering where you'd gone, that's all." He had no intention of mentioning strange hallucinations. "Let's go into the other room; it's creepy in here."

Shakily Kate followed him. She couldn't believe it. Had she only been in the back storeroom a little while?

She stared at her watch. It wasn't even four o'clock. Yet surely she'd been with Wadat for days, a timeless disembodied spirit following him through the wilderness, sensing his communion with the eagle, touching the stone along with him and Hizu.

Quickly she thrust a hand into her pocket. The stone was there. The same red stone with the three grooves. She began to tremble as if she had a fever. There was no way she could go on like this. She had to tell someone about it, maybe even Jimmy. But no, he'd think she was crazy. Anyone would. Maybe she was. Yet there must be something she could do. Was this stone possessing her, driving her crazy for no purpose at all?

Kate closed the storeroom door behind her and suddenly knew there was one thing she could do. What had Hizu said? Carve the design into a large stone. And he once must have done the same with his own design.

"Jimmy," she said as she seated herself at the table again, "do you know much about petroglyph designs?"

"A little, I suppose."

"Well, there's this one pattern. . . . I saw it somewhere, and I think it must be a petroglyph design. It's not at Indian Cliffs though, and I was wondering if you had any idea where it might be."

"What's it like?"

"Well, it's . . . Here, I'd better draw it." Kate took up a pencil and tore a blank page from Jimmy's notebook. Then she sat down and tried to conjure up the pattern again. She'd seen it often enough when she hadn't wanted to. Closing her eyes she waited, and slowly it began to form in the darkness. She concentrated on it as she never had before, and then, opening her eyes, began to trace the outline onto paper.

At last, exhausted, she ran a hand over her face and looked down at the paper. Yes, that was it exactly. The circle was slightly squashed, as was the spiral inside, and the outside spokes jutted at different angles.

Kate pushed the paper across the table. "Ever seen that before?"

Jimmy picked up the paper and studied it. "Well, it's got a lot of common elements. It sure looks like it could be a petroglyph design. I wonder. . . . Is that the museum's library over there?" He pointed to a couple of dust-laden bookshelves.

"What there is of it, I guess."

"Well, there's one book that is bound to be there." Jimmy walked over, scanned the shelf, then grunted with satisfaction. He returned carrying a big tan book and plunked it on the table. "It's been revised since this edition, but most of the material's the same. These guys did a survey of the state's big petroglyph sites, and there're a lot of pictures."

He pulled his chair next to Kate's, and slowly they began turning page after page of sketches. Circles, zigzags, ovals, ladders, crisscrosses, animals. The designs were endless, mesmerizing.

Suddenly Kate jerked. "There." She jammed a finger down on a page.

Jimmy pulled the book toward him. "Boy, you sure have a photographic memory. You've got it down to the last squiggle. Where'd you see it?"

"Oh, I don't know exactly. But where is it, on the rock, I mean?"

"Hmm," Jimmy looked at the number and letter code under the drawing. "This one's at Tanner River. Oh, that's a great site. I've been there."

"Can I go there?"

"You sure can't walk. It's not as near as Indian Cliffs."

"Well, are there buses that go near it?"

"Heck no. It's way out in the middle of nowhere. My brother George and I went by motorcycle. It's not a real powerful model, but it's all fixed up for off-road."

Kate looked down at her clenched hands. She'd never had anything harder to say in her life, or anything she needed to say more. "Will you take me there?"

"Will I . . . ? Hey, Kate, that's asking a little much, don't you think?"

"Yes, yes, I guess so. But I've got to go there."

"Maybe, but I've got to work at the restaurant. I can't go driving off over the countryside with a girl whose got a bee in her bonnet about Indian petroglyphs."

"If you do, I'll get Mom to let you come here every day to research."

"I'd like that, sure, but . . ."

"And if you don't, I'll see that you never get to come here again."

"Hey, that's not fair. And this is a public museum anyway. You can't keep me out."

"I can tell my mom you stole something today and shouldn't ever be let in again."

Jimmy stood up so quickly his chair tipped over.

"That'd be a mean lie! I'd never steal anything, and you know it!"

Kate was almost reduced to tears by now. "Yes, yes, I know. But I've just got to go to that site! You've no idea how much it means to me. I'll do anything, really."

Jimmy sat back down. "Okay, but let's be businesslike again. No lies about my stealing anything. Otherwise, I won't help you at all."

Kate nodded, wishing she weren't acting like such a fool, but she was desperate.

"My brother left me the bike when he went off to college. I use it around here some, but to and from Tanner River, with some time for exploring, that'd take at least three days. It's ridiculous anyway. My parents would never let me do it."

"Tell them it's your gateway to archaeological eminence. A real feather in your cap. You'll be given limitless access to the Argentum Indian collection."

"Somehow I don't think that will move them much." He grinned. "But it does me. I'll try." He returned the book to its shelf. "Want me to call you once I get the word from them?"

Kate thought of the satisfied look on her mother's face if she answered a call for Kate—from a boy. "No. Let's meet at some neutral site."

"Businesslike to the end. All right. A neutral site. How about the school yard?"

"Right. At the same time tomorrow, two o'clock."

Jimmy began putting away the artifacts he'd been studying. "I'm not sure it's a pleasure doing business with you, Kate Elliot, but it is interesting."

SEVEN

KATE LEANED BACK AGAINST THE WEATHERED brick wall, cool in its narrow two o'clock shadow. The rest of the playground was sun-battered and bright. Nothing moved but a few scraps of paper skittering across the packed dirt on a hot dry wind.

She certainly didn't want to be seen meeting secretly with a boy. But out in the open though this was, it was still a good place for a rendezvous. Nothing was more invisible than a school in summer. Adults never notice schools anyway; they're part of an alien world. And kids live their summers with the fiction that such places don't exist. No one even came to use the playground equipment, the metal bars and swinging horses that shone blisteringly hot in the summer sun.

Something was moving now, besides blown trash. Way down the road someone was walking toward her. Jimmy. Kate's throat tightened. She didn't want this, she didn't want his help. But she needed it.

All last night her dreams had been pierced by that haunting flute tune. Today the spiral pattern had glittered almost everywhere, and even now she could feel two charm stones, one in each pocket. She'd almost gotten used to it, carrying around two stones, one real and one that wasn't there. She wondered if lunatics eventually got used to their lunacy. She shuddered.

At one point last night, she'd almost decided to climb back up to Indian Cliffs and bury the stone where she'd found it. But she knew that wouldn't work. It would probably come slithering down the gully after her and appear in the drawer with her father's letters, lying on the top one perhaps, the one that talked about how the world needed her.

Besides, the stone she actually had wasn't really the problem. It was the other one, Hizu's stone, the black one with the spiral groove. Going back to the petroglyph rock that had the three scars wouldn't help. It wasn't that pattern that was tormenting her. She had to find some big rock with that horrid spiral pattern. She didn't know why, but if there was an answer anywhere, it had to be there.

Suddenly Jimmy was trudging across the playground looking hot and annoyed. He plunked himself onto the shadowed ground at the foot of the wall. "My parents say no," he said flatly.

Kate felt her mind crumbling. "They can't have."

"They could and they did. My dad said I had to get this archaeology stuff out of my head, and he wasn't going to let me go off into the wilds with a young lady. My mother tried. She said that even a restaurateur needs a hobby, that Dad was being stuffy and old-fashioned, and that Kate Elliot seemed like a nice girl and she was sure that our interests were purely academic. But Dad said it was a matter of family duty and honor and that was that."

Kate slumped down to the ground beside him. Misery and anger brimmed over into hysteria. "People. I hate them!"

"Hey, some of us aren't so bad."

"No, they all are. My dad was okay, but he wanted to help people and he died. I never even got to tell him I loved him, and now he's gone, and I wish I hadn't loved him anyway, because then it wouldn't hurt so much."

Her face was red and teary, and somehow she just couldn't stop. "People are hateful. They always hurt you or make demands on you. I thought the old Indians would be safe, they'd be good and dead. But they're worse than the others. They demand and demand, but I don't know what they're demanding!"

She stood up. "I hate them. I don't want anything to do with them." Suddenly she reached into her pocket. "Here. I can't throw it away; maybe I can give it away. Take it, add it to your precious collection. I never want to see it again—or you. Get out of here!"

Eyes wide with confusion, Jimmy took the stone from her hand. He stood up. "Hey, I'm sorry. I—"

"Don't be sorry. I don't want to know you—or anybody. Particularly them. Get away from me!"

Jimmy felt as if he were facing a rabid animal. "Okay. Thanks for the stone. But you can have it back if you feel better later." He really didn't want to see her again, though. She was crazy. He turned and walked across the playground as fast as dignity would allow.

Kate leaned back against the wall, shaking and

breathing in ragged sobs. She had just gone completely mad. Jimmy was sure to send the guys with straight jackets after her. Or he should. Poor guy. He had tried to help, and she'd gone crazy on him and given him that stone. That was like giving a person poison. Well, at least she was rid of it.

She slumped again to the ground and propped her head on her knees. Or was she? She'd placed that one stone, the real one, in his hand, but the other was still with her, a nonexistent lump in her pocket. She'd never get rid of that one, and now the stones would be driving two Argentum kids crazy. It wasn't right. They shouldn't meddle in people's lives like that, those stones. She wouldn't let them!

Kate jumped to her feet, trying to smear away the tears from her face. She'd go after Jimmy now and tell him everything. Then if he didn't believe her, at least he'd be warned. She'd be rid of that, at least.

As soon as the school building was out of sight, Jimmy broke into a run. Boy, he didn't know what Kate's problem was, but she sure had one. It was hardly fair, his taking the stone from her. She clearly wasn't thinking straight. It sure was a terrific piece, though.

He slowed to a walk and unclenched his hand. The tapered, red stone lay smooth and cool on his palm. Slowly with one finger, he traced the three curved grooves. Perfect. The nicest thing in his collection. If he kept it, that is. He shouldn't, though. He'd give Kate some time, then he'd offer it back. Maybe she wouldn't take it. She sure was strange.

He looked up. He'd been thinking so hard, he hadn't

paid attention to where he was going. Taken a wrong turn somewhere, though how he could do that in this little town he couldn't imagine. Still, he was out of town entirely. In front of him was a hillside and a boy sitting on a rock.

Jimmy didn't recognize the kid, a tourist probably. He certainly was dressed strangely enough. An old-fashioned hippie maybe. Jimmy was about to turn away when he noticed something the boy was holding. Jimmy took a few steps closer.

The boy had ruddy skin and straight black hair. He wasn't wearing much except for dangly beads and some sort of leatherish-looking pants. But that didn't matter. It was what he held in his hand that Jimmy noticed.

Sitting cross-legged on a rock and turned mostly away from Jimmy, the boy was examining the contents of a leather bag. There was a dark feather, a gold-flecked pebble, and a smooth reddish stone. Tapered at both ends, it was marked with three curved grooves.

Jimmy took another step, then stared down at the exact same stone in his own hand. He gasped. At the sound the boy looked around. Jimmy saw three curved scars on his face, a face he had seen once before—in that flashing vision at the museum.

Suddenly Jimmy felt something hurtle into him. He was twisted sideways and smashed to the ground. Noise blared angrily. His chin hurt.

Voices came from all around him. "Fool kid!" "Is he hurt?" "She saved his life, did you see that?" "Someone get a doctor, for goodness sakes!"

VISION QUEST

Jimmy blinked at the asphalt. He hadn't been on a paved road. He'd been out of town. And why was he lying down like this anyway? Somebody was kneeling beside him.

"It's okay, Jimmy," Kate's voice whispered. "Don't tell them what you saw. Just say you were thinking of something else." Kate and others helped him to his feet.

"What do you mean," an angry man said, "just sauntering out into the highway like that? You high on something, kid?"

"Oh, leave him alone," a woman snapped. "Why, that car would have hit him if this girl hadn't pushed him out of the way. You're Bernie Grant's niece, aren't you? And you, I believe, young man, are one of the Fong boys."

"Yes, ma'am," Jimmy said, giving Kate a bewildered look. "I'm sorry. I . . . I guess I wasn't looking where I was going."

More solicitous people asked if he was all right, and then a couple of them helped him home. The doctor came, looked him over, and pronounced him healthy except for a scraped chin, a twisted knee, and a little shock. He gave him something, and Jimmy slept through the rest of the day and night.

Next morning, Kate visited him. When she was alone with Jimmy in the room, she pulled up a chair beside the bed. "I didn't see what you saw, but I can guess. Will you tell me?"

"I will, if you explain all this to me."

Kate smiled sheepishly. "Yeah. Another deal. I really

should have explained before, and I never should have given you that stone. That's why I was following you. I felt guilty."

"Look, I don't get it. I wander out of town and there's this strange kid sitting on a hillside holding exactly the same stone. And suddenly you knock me to the street out of the way of a car that I swear wasn't there a moment earlier. What gives?"

"You were really in town all along, Jimmy. You wandered out into the street while you thought you were looking at Wadat, that's the boy's name. He and the hillside were really there, too, only a long time ago."

"Which of us fell down and hit our head?"

"Will you let me explain?"

He did. Kate was just finishing when Mrs. Fong came in to say that Jimmy needed rest. Kate agreed. He looked as if he'd just been hit on the head a second time.

On her way home, three people stopped Kate on the street to praise her heroism in saving Jimmy Fong's life. Blushing, she mumbled her thanks, more thankful still that they'd never know the truth. She was incredibly relieved though that Jimmy knew it. And she might as well stop feeling guilty about not telling him before. He'd probably never have believed a word if this hadn't happened to him.

Next morning she was back visiting the invalid. The scab on his chin looked gross, like a glob of dried jam, he suggested. His knee was getting better though, and he could get up and hobble around the room. He was more interested in talking than walking, however.

"Well," he said after shooing out his sisters and brothers, "after what you told me yesterday, I put that stone way over on the windowsill, about as far away as I could. But I still kept hearing this funny little tune. Didn't see any lights, though."

Kate nodded. "You probably won't. You never touched the other stone, Hizu's stone."

"Anyway, I can see why you want to get to Tanner River and find that rock with the spiral petroglyph. Though how exactly that will help . . ."

"I know. It's just that I can't think of anything else to do. And I can't go on with this other world dropping in and out on me."

"You can say that again. I could have been killed right here on Juniper Street while I thought I was on a bare hillside watching that Wadat kid."

Kate frowned for a minute, then asked, "How do you suppose all this works? Do we keep jumping back to the past, or is it that both are going on at the same time, somehow?"

"Don't know. But once I heard a guy on the radio say that time is like a river, things only seem to be passing if you're on it. But to anyone up high enough, it's all one thing, all happening at the same time."

Kate thought a moment. "So maybe this, whatever, sort of takes us up and lets us look at two things, two times at once."

"Something like that, maybe."

Suddenly Kate remembered the eagle, Wadat's eagle, with all the hills, valleys, and streams spread at once beneath its wings. Spirit wings.

For a while the two sat in silence, then Kate spoke. "So what are we going to do? I mean, to keep from going crazy or being massacred on the roads."

"I've got an idea. No guarantees, but maybe I can work something out." He grinned. "Purely a professional arrangement, you understand."

Knots seemed to loosen inside of her. She grinned back. "Of course."

Two nights later, the phone rang at Kate's house. Her mother looked insufferably pleased when she handed the phone over, but Kate hardly cared. So what that Jimmy Fong was a friend? She needed a friend. It was worth the risk.

"It's okay," his voice said over the receiver. "My dad says that now family honor can only be upheld if I do my benefactor a good deed in return. We can go to Tanner River."

EIGHT

WINNING PERMISSION FOR THE TRIP ON KATE'S SIDE was almost as difficult but less dramatic. At first her mother was opposed, but Uncle Bernie intervened. Kate overheard him arguing that this was the first real social contact that Kate had had in Argentum. Jimmy Fong was a good, levelheaded kid (ignoring the incident on the street); he knew the country and always drove his motorcycle carefully. To the complaint that gossiping tongues might wag, Bernie pointed out that it would take a lot of scandalizing to erase Kate's current image as a heroine. This was their chance to have Kate get to know both the people and the land. Kate's mother held out awhile longer but finally gave in. After all, she admitted, this was the first time in a long while that Kate had actually *wanted* to do anything or to be with anyone.

So early on a Friday morning, Kate sat in front of the house, a bulging pack at her side. She rather wished she hadn't eavesdropped on all that discussion about herself. But she guessed it didn't matter so much why she was being allowed to go on this trip as long as nobody guessed the real reason for it. Then both she and Jimmy would be sent to the Nevada State Nuthouse, for sure.

Leaning back against a gatepost, she watched the sky, calm and pale with dawn. Sun gilded the highest peak, but below, cold night air still lay pooled between the mountains. The stillness was broken by a distant growl that sounded like a soprano bear. Quickly it came nearer.

Soon the bike sputtered to a halt in front of her, spewing up a modest spray of dust. Kate was on her feet at once, taking it all in.

"Well, you certainly look the part," she said, eyeing Jimmy's black leather jacket and featureless black helmet.

Jimmy flipped up the face plate and grinned. "Yeah, and I've got a matching outfit for you." In a moment, he was handing her a second jacket and helmet, which he'd hooked to the back of his pack.

"Come on, do you want me to look like some sort of urban terrorist?"

"Hey, there's a good reason for a leather jacket. If you fall off a motorcycle in a cloth jacket, you'll leave half your skin behind on the road. Leather protects you. And nobody rides with me without a helmet."

"All right, all right, but is this sinister dark visor necessary? I'll look like Darth Vader."

"Suit yourself, but the wind and glare get pretty fierce. Come on, let's load up. I want to be well on our way before it gets too hot."

Kate's pack was soon strapped to the back, and she

seated herself on the long black seat behind the driver. Even with the jacket and helmet on, she felt fragile and exposed. She could imagine her mother running out screaming that it was far too dangerous for her little girl to ride around like that. The thought gave her courage.

"Hold on," Jimmy called through his helmet. Kate had no intention of grabbing his waist—until he kicked the machine into life and it shot down the hill. Then, clutching on for dear life, she decided he was just a convenient hand grip.

Wind whipped at her face, exhilarating and fresh. Jimmy had said that his bike was old and pokey, but to her the speed seemed giddy, as fast as the wind itself. The morning-dark buildings swept by in a blur, giving way to rocks and trees, as the highway cut down out of the mountains toward the broad sweeping valley.

Suddenly the bike swerved slightly, and the speed slowed. Gripping tighter, Kate peered ahead. A group of hikers was walking down the road, seemingly oblivious to any possible traffic. Jimmy raised his hand to the bike's horn but never pressed it. One more look and Kate knew why. The hikers had no T-shirts, no dark glasses, no bright vinyl packs. And where they walked, there was no road, only a foot path and a rocky ravine. In moments the noisy bike was up to them and through them, but not one browned body flinched or dark head turned their way. Only a single pair of eyes met hers, those of a lone boy. Then they were past.

Kate didn't want to look around. She knew the ravine would be empty. A bare paved road would stretch up toward the huddled town. In her pockets, where this morning she had placed one stone, the two of them now felt solid and heavy.

Jimmy raised his visor and turned back to her. "How about wrapping that stone in vision-proof foil. It's a hazard to navigation."

She laughed weakly, but there was nothing to say.

"Oh, well," Jimmy continued, his attention back on the road. "At least we're on the right trail."

Kate too turned her attention back to the scenery. She finally had to lower her visor against the wind and glare, but although the tone darkened, the picture hardly changed. It was stark and wild. Except for the road, she doubted if the two of them would notice if they shifted from one time to another. The mark of modern man on this land was very slight.

The valley into which they dropped glowed with dawn. Blue-green sage filled it like a misty sea and lapped at the base of the distant mountains. To the north and south, the valley stretched into the hazy distance, but at its western edge, mountains rose in a purple wall that seemed to blend with the sky. Their snow-whitened peaks looked more like low clouds.

And there were real clouds. The sky was a clear sharp blue and vastly high. Yet, here and there clouds towered into it, piled one on top of another, the pueblos of distant sky gods.

The road stretched across the valley, like a rope sagging in the middle, then slowly rising again. Antlike, a few vehicles traveled along it, a truck, several cars, a pair of far grander-looking motorcycles. After their own bike rose to another pass, Jimmy stopped, consulted a map, then left the highway.

VISION QUEST

The road he chose was not paved. Gravel had been halfheartedly strewn over the first mile, then this gave way to rutted, packed dirt. There was enough solid surface for the single wheels of the cycle, but Jimmy imagined an ordinary car would have a tough time of it.

Laboriously they climbed through a gap of tumbled rock, then found themselves in a long high valley. Mountain peaks ran along its edges, some gently folded, some jagged and dramatic. The sky rose above them, and ahead stretched sage and grass unmarred by fences, buildings, or anything but the pale scar of the road.

After awhile Jimmy stopped for lunch. Their engine sputtered out, and silence fell on them, vast and total.

Even the slight clatter they made as they rummaged through packs seemed intrusive. Jimmy handed Kate a can of deviled ham, then pulled out a box of crackers. "This route's pretty wild, but it's a lot shorter. And there's not much traffic except for range cows."

"I can see why."

He grinned. "Don't worry, we'll hit another highway in a bit. Civilization's not totally lost."

They settled into the shade of a gnarled juniper, quietly eating and watching the clouds. Some of the white spires they had seen earlier had now hardened into rain clouds. At one end of the valley, cloud-shadows had turned the mountain peaks into stark, flat cutouts, silver black silhouettes against a pale gray sky. From some clouds, rain fell in dark veils, most of which vanished in the dry air before even touching the ground.

Despite herself, Kate felt awed. "It really is beautiful. It almost looks like a jigsaw puzzle." Immediately she blushed. Now Jimmy would think the only spectacular scenery she'd ever seen was on a puzzle box. But he didn't seem to catch that.

"Yeah, but with my luck I'd probably get to do that bit over there where everything's all gray. Let's get going."

They mounted up and continued down the valley, drawing nearer and nearer to the rain clouds. Soon they could hear thunder rolling between the peaks. Lightning cracked the sky in thin jagged bolts. Wind blew one of the rain curtains toward them, and the air smelled of damp earth and tangy wet sage.

Jimmy steered the cycle off the road and jounced toward some piled rocks. He slowed and stopped.

"These desert storms are mostly local," he said over a new rumble of thunder, "but I think this one's going to hit us. Let's wait it out under this rock. No use getting all our stuff soaked."

They rolled the cycle as close as they could to the rock overhang, then unstrapped their bags. The first large drops of rain were splatting into the dust as they scrambled under shelter. Pressing back against the rough surface, they watched the wind-whipped rain sweep in sheets across the valley while lightning stabbed again and again through the sky. The boulders around them shook with thunder.

Then they became aware, both together, that they were not alone in the shelter. Kate slipped the red stone from her pocket. She almost wanted to throw it out into the rain, to wash it clean of what it was bringing. Yet there was a need that held it in her hand. Jimmy's hand closed over hers.

A third person was crouching among the rocks. His hands pressed against fresh carvings on its surface, seeking comfort where there was none. The sound of his sobbing replaced the thunder, and his thoughts moved softly into theirs. The boy's eyes blurred with tears. He didn't want to see the rocks or the carvings around him; he wanted to see Hizu. And he never would again.

Memories choked him worse than the tears. For almost a year after his vision quest, he had lived with the old man, learning the medicine plants, the chants, and the ways of the spirits. Often they had traveled alone, just the two of them, living off what food they could find, the roots and grubs or the unwary animals that the spirits sent their way. Sometimes, too, they stopped with groups of people, people who were happy to have a shaman join them.

But that is where the trouble had come. Sick people sought out Hizu's aid, but not everyone got well. Yomeninaku, known among many bands as a great hunter, was ill with terrible pains in his stomach. Hizu chanted over him and danced, fell into a trance, and tried to draw forth the illness with feathers and healing stones. But all in vain. The strong hunter died in terrible pain.

Word of this failure spread more swiftly than sage fire, and other families took in the traveling shaman less willingly. Then several bands gathered together for a rabbit hunt. It was a disaster. Scarcely one rabbit ran into the nets. This might have been the fault of Hizu's hunting magic; it might have been due to the loss of Yomeninaku the hunter. But either way, the blame clearly fell on the old shaman. The spirits had deserted him, the people muttered, and would desert them all if he stayed among them. No people could survive in this land without the spirits' aid.

It frightened Wadat to hear people whispering against his friend. He urged the old man to leave, to go with him alone into the mountains, to talk with the spirits and not with these foolish frightened people. But Hizu would not go. He said all things have a season, a beginning and an end.

One cool fall evening, the people gathered for a scanty meal around their fire. Sage smoke climbed up toward the young pale stars. But Wadat could watch only Hizu, who sat chewing slowly, seemingly unaware of the storm of feeling building around him. Everyone else averted their gaze from the old man.

Then three men stepped out of the dusk and stood beside Hizu. They said nothing, but the old shaman put down his bowl and stood up to join them. Briefly, his eye caught Wadat's. He patted his side where his medicine bag usually hung, yet oddly it was not there. Then he turned and walked with the others into the gathering darkness.

Wadat trembled. He wanted to scream, to rush after them, to stop them. A hand gripped his shoulder. It was his aunt. She looked at him with hushing, downcast eyes.

He could not follow, he knew. He could do nothing. This was the way of his people. But he could not stay at that silent meal a moment longer. Wadat stood and ran off, away from all that was happening. He would have sped like an endlessly hunted rabbit, but suddenly he remembered.

Hizu had sought his eyes and had patted the place where his medicine bag usually hung. Abruptly Wadat changed course and ran to where he and Hizu had made their sleeping place. There Wadat knelt and raised an edge of the old man's tattered rabbit fur blanket. Swiftly he felt beneath. His fingers touched it, the medicine bag. Tenderly he pulled it out. His throat tightened. He knew what he must do.

"Give that to me," a voice said in the darkness. Wadat jumped to his feet, clutching the bag to him. His uncle stood before him. He had been one of the three men.

"No, I can not. These are his medicine things. I must treat them properly, or his spirit can never be at rest."

The other's voice was cold. "He *will* never be at rest. He is a failed shaman. Such a one can not live among our people without bringing evil upon them. His body must abandon life then be scattered over the land, and so must his things of power. Otherwise his spirit will seek vengeance and do our people harm."

"He would never do anyone harm!" Wadat cried, his voice high with despair. "He was a good man, a wise man. My friend."

"Wadat, you know nothing. Give me that bag."

"His charm stone, then. Let me take that. A shaman's

81

stone must be buried at the rock carved with his spirit sign."

"He is no shaman! His memory is shunned, his name will never again pass our lips." The man struck like a snake and snatched the bag away. "*You* are our shaman now, strange as that seems. You are all the aid that the spirits have granted us. Go and speak with them, boy. They should teach you what is proper."

The man vanished into the darkness, taking the precious, soul-binding stone. In anguish, Wadat turned toward the hills. Running at first, then walking blindly, he wandered for days seeking guidance of the spirits. But his mind and heart were too troubled for any spirit to speak to him.

Finally he came to rocks, the same rocks where Hizu had carved his last spirit drawing, the charm for that final failed hunt.

Wadat slumped to the ground below it and wept. Hizu would never walk with him again. Even his spirit would be lost. It could never join as it should with the rocks and trees and living things of the earth. Even the barest shaman's ritual had been denied him, the uniting of his spirit stones. People die to become one with the land, yet Hizu never would. And now he, Wadat, would never find his friend in the land, he would never have the comfort of hearing his voice in the wind, or of seeing his loving glance in the eyes of a desert owl.

This should not be! Surely the spirits of this land would listen. Otherwise, how could he serve them well, how could he live with this unquenchable grief? Somehow surely the spirits would bring help.

VISION QUEST

His sobbing subsided at last, and Wadat curled up like a spent animal. The tears dried from his eyes, leaving them red and aching. He opened them, and for a brief lightning flash, he met other eyes staring into his.

NINE

THE STORM HAD PASSED. OUTSIDE THE ROCK shelter, the world sparkled like new washed crystal. The air rising from the damp earth was unbearably sharp and fresh.

Jimmy and Kate stumbled into it, blinking in the clear bright light. They gazed around with a mixture of confusion and clarity. For all of their drifting through time and memory, it seemed that only minutes had passed.

Finally Jimmy spoke. "Well, at least we have a little better idea of what has to be done."

"We do?"

"Sure . . . I think. Hizu's charm stone needs to be buried under the rock with the sun sign on it. Isn't that it?"

"Yes, maybe. But we don't have his stone, we have Wadat's." She opened her hand, and the red stone glowed warmly in the sun. Looking at it, she wished again she'd never taken it. And yet she didn't feel as frightened as she had before. True, old spirits were appearing to them, yet the term *haunting* didn't seem right. Was it haunting if another human being was asking for help?

84

VISION QUEST

That phrase made her stiffen; echoes of her father's creed, the one that had killed him. Still, she was choosing what she was doing, and she could choose not to do it any time she wished.

Jimmy had been pursuing his own thoughts. Now he walked to the motorcycle and began wheeling it toward the road. "Well, whichever stone we have, it looks like the only thing we can do is go on to Tanner River. Maybe something will . . . come to us there."

Soon Kate was seated behind Jimmy, and they were off again jouncing down the rutted road. But her mind kept returning to his last remark. "Something will come to us." Another vision perhaps? She shivered. Leading one life's worth of problems was hard enough; she didn't need to take on someone else's. Just as she didn't need spirits or whatever meddling with things—particularly if she was one of those things.

Still, resent it as she might, she couldn't deny that this whole business was effecting her. Even now the thoughts she had shared with Wadat left her feeling empty and sad. They had been so close, Wadat and the old man. Hizu had loved him, taught him, acted as a father to him. Then he'd been torn away and killed, and Wadat had been helpless even to fulfill his last request, to properly bury his shaman stone and send his spirit home to the land.

Pain of loss and frustration gripped Kate suddenly, as fresh and raw as when she'd heard of her own father's death. Again she wanted to cry out, as Wadat had done—a cry that had lingered here for countless years, perhaps simply waiting to be heard. She wavered between horror and acceptance. But still, she had heard it, and now couldn't help but answer—or try to.

Their dirt track soon skirted the mountains at the end of the valley and joined a paved road. They turned west. The sun was low over the mountains now. Kate wished they could get to that river place tonight, but recalling the map, she knew they couldn't make it. That meant camping out somewhere beside the road, and she really didn't like that idea.

You're a wimp city girl, she told herself, but that did not help. The cold, the dirt, and the hard ground did not appeal; but what she really hated, she admitted to herself, was trying to find someplace private enough to go to the bathroom, then squatting there and worrying about scorpions and such coming up from behind. Wimp!

Now they were part of a thin flow of traffic: a few cars, a few trucks, an occasional camper. Kate liked this comfortable touch of civilization. Then, when they stopped at a crossroads for gas, she noticed a sign that said CAMPING. It pointed off to a grove of cottonwoods.

She tugged at Jimmy's arm. "Let's stay there tonight."

"At a commercial camp? You've got to be kidding. It'll be jammed with RVs and screaming kids and folks so afraid of the wild they've got to play their tape players full blast. Yippy little dogs, smelly latrines. You don't want a commercial camp."

"Hmm. Well, couldn't we just go and look it over? Maybe we could use the facilities, take a shower? Then if we don't want to stay, we can go on and find a place of our own."

"All right, all right. A shower doesn't sound so bad. I've got dust ground into every pore."

VISION QUEST

The camp was fairly full by the time they arrived. There weren't many campgrounds in this part of the state, and this one seemed to have filled up early with those noisy urban campers Jimmy had predicted.

They left the cycle at a small litter-strewn campsite and went to check out and use the other facilities before deciding whether to stay. There were latrines and beside them a shower building. The shower was rather run-down looking, Kate thought, but she felt so gritty she would have willingly stood in the spray of a fire hydrant. The water was only lukewarm, heated by the sun beating all day on the pipes. Still, it felt heavenly.

Feeling considerably better about life, she walked out of the women's side of the building, only to stop and suddenly jump back behind the partition. She bumped into a soft jiggly woman in tight pink shorts, but ignored the squawk of complaint.

What mattered was the man she'd seen walking toward the building: large, bushy red beard, a white towel thrown over his shoulder. Peering through the slats in the wooden partition, she watched him disappear into the man's side of the building. She refused to consider what sort of supernatural meddling might have brought this chance about. The point was, it was too good a chance to pass up.

Kate sprinted back to the campsite. Jimmy was there looking scrubbed, sitting on his sleeping bag, grudgingly filling out one of the camp forms.

"I've seen him! He's here!" she said breathlessly.

"Who? Bigfoot? The president of the United States? Maybe . . ."

"Stow it. It's Pete the pothunter. He just went in to take a shower. If he's here with his artifact van, the stone could still be in it!"

Jimmy jumped up. "Can you recognize the van?"

"Couldn't miss it. It's black with stenciled red flames. Really tacky."

It didn't take them long to find the van. And though it wasn't very well screened from the rest of the camp, they figured it was already dark enough to conceal a break-in. With Kate on one side of the van and Jimmy on the other, they tried doors and windows.

Kate found everything on her side locked tight. She was just walking around to check the back doors when she heard a squeal from Jimmy's side. Then a voice.

"All right, kid, what do you think you're doing?"

"Nothing, sir. Just looking at your van. It, eh, sure is terrific, sir."

"Don't 'sir' me. You were trying to break in, you thieving little gook. If I catch you here again, I'll skin you. Shove off."

"I certainly will not bother you again, sir," Jimmy said stiffly. "But you called me a gook, a pejorative term for Vietnamese. I am not Vietnamese. I am Chinese."

"All right. You thieving little chink, then. Now get the hell out of here!"

From her hiding place, Kate heard the sound of hastily retreating footsteps. Stealthily, she slipped into the trees before Pete could catch her, too. From there she sped back to their campsite. Jimmy was already there, looking shaken.

"What a beast," she said. "He ought to have his mouth scrubbed with particularly nasty soap."

"Hey, it's not the names I mind. It's being picked up and shaken like a wet towel. If I was about two hundred pounds heavier, I'd go shake him up a bit."

"Good. I bet you know karate."

"Hey, what is it with everybody? I'm not Japanese, either. I'm *Chinese.*"

"Okay, okay. So what have you got going for you then? How about sage advice. Any words of wisdom from Confucius or somebody?"

Jimmy sighed. "Hopeless. Okay, how about 'There's more than one way to skin a cat'?"

"Doesn't sound very oriental."

"Sorry. I've never been farther east than Salt Lake City. But the translation is, if we can't break in now, we can wait till our friend's asleep and try later. We can't lose a chance like this."

It was almost dark now, but far from quiet. In the trailer next door, a couple was arguing loudly, while on the other side people were drinking beer and singing along with loud songs on their tape player. Small children bawled from different parts of the camp, and dogs yipped back and forth at each other.

Kate and Jimmy took turns walking slowly up the road to check on Pete's campsite. At first they were afraid he'd sleep in his van, but at last they saw him set up a small green tent a few yards away and crawl inside.

The campground noises had subsided by then, but it was far from a silent desert night. Trying not to step on crackling branches, the two crept through the band of trees backing the campsites, then eased their way toward the van. A wheezy rumbling, steady and reassuring, came from the tent on the other side of the van.

Scarcely breathing, Kate pulled out a flashlight and, covering all but a thin beam with her hand, lighted a collection of oddments Jimmy had pulled from his pocket. They'd assembled everything that looked useful for lock picking: a hairpin, a piece of wire, the key off the sardine can from dinner, and various tools Jimmy had brought in case the cycle needed repairing.

One after another they tried these on the van's back door. Nothing worked. Finally Kate whispered she'd go back and get her key chain. It had her mom's extra car key, and the make was the same as the van's. Worth trying, anyway.

Sneaking back through the trees, she was halfway to their camp when she heard a snarl like a triumphant lion. "You again, you slant-eyed little vandal. I'm hauling you to the camp manager, and he'll call the police."

Kate turned and ran back so noisily she didn't hear Jimmy's squeaked reply. She arrived in time to see a tall burly figure dragging a small thrashing one out onto the campground road. Running forward, she grabbed a fallen branch and hurled it with all her strength at the man's head.

Roaring indignantly, he let go of his captive and raised both hands to his bald spot. Jimmy pelted off like a rabbit; Pete followed in yelling pursuit. They tore through several campsites before the big man tripped over a guy-wire and sprawled onto a small tent. Its occupants emerged with threats and cursing, which Pete, struggling to his feet, returned in kind.

Neighbors shouted "shut up," and dogs had hysterics as Kate walked calmly down the road. Reaching her own campsite, she hopped fully clothed into her sleeping bag and listened to the angry noises gradually subside. Eventually through the emerging silence, she heard someone creep up to the empty sleeping bag beside her and crawl in.

"Thanks," a voice whispered in the dark. "A very good shot."

"And you led him a good chase. He's a clumsy oaf, to say nothing of a major bigot."

"Yeah. 'Slant-eyed vandal,' indeed. The Vandals were a European tribe, definitely not oriental."

Kate snorted. "So you don't mind a bigot, only an inaccurate one."

"Right. It offends my eminent scholarliness. Now, let's forget it, all of it, and get some sleep."

TEN

THE STAR-STREWN BLACKNESS WAS FADING TO gray when Kate felt someone poking her. "We'd better get going," Jimmy whispered. "I really don't want our friend to see me again even though we need to see *him.*"

Silently, they rolled up their bags, stowed their gear on the back of the cycle, then wheeled it down to where the campground road joined the highway. There they hid behind a clump of yucca and sage, shared a couple of granola bars, and settled down to wait.

The air was cold, so Kate zipped her jacket to the top. She sat cross-legged on the hard dusty ground, staring not so much at the road as at the flowers and bushes that screened it. The flowers had pale blue-gray stems and tiny white starlike blossoms. They smelled sharp and sweet, like cough medicine.

"What kind of flowers are those, Jimmy?"

"Don't know. I'm an Indian specialist. My mom's into flowers though; she can name dozens and dozens of them. I just call them the orange ones, the purple ones, the white ones. Except I can tell you what that one is."

He pointed to a spot beside Kate where a cluster of fat spiny cactus ears had burst into feathery red flowers.

"Brilliant," Kate said, shifting herself slightly. "Noted botanist identifies cactus."

Their attention snapped back to the road as a large silver camper swayed down to the highway. It was followed a few minutes later by an athletic-looking young couple on bicycles.

"Duck!" Jimmy said suddenly. Kate flattened herself behind the sage and peered through the shaggy stems as the black van rolled past. Slowly she swiveled around and watched as it turned west onto the highway and picked up speed.

"Follow that van!" Jimmy shouted, springing towards the motorcycle.

"Not too close," Kate cautioned. "If he recognizes you, he might open up with a machine gun."

Jimmy rolled the cycle onto the highway. "That's the advantage of these sinister space-invader helmets. I could be a blond Norwegian as easily as a thieving slant-eyed Vandal."

Soon they were shooting down the highway again, but it became clear that Kate needn't have worried about getting too close. Jimmy's cycle steadily dropped behind their quarry. Finally the van was lost from sight as the road ahead bent around a bare arm of mountain. When they reached that point, there were several more bends to come, and the van was nowhere to be seen.

"What are we going to do?" Kate called over the hot driving wind.

"Keep heading west. It's not the way to Tanner River,

but if there's any chance of tracking down that stone, we ought to try."

Kate settled into the monotony of motion and scenery watching. Without much effort, she could imagine herself mounted on "Old Paint," riding through endless Western movies, pursuing lost cattle or desperate outlaws.

She hated to admit it, but she could almost see how someone could like this country, how it could get into your blood. It had a sort of raw appeal, just earth and rocks and baking sun, with not even enough of the dry, brittle vegetation to cover it.

Where she'd been in the East and Midwest, plants grew so quickly that you never saw the earth except at construction sites or plowed fields. And there were so many trees, bushes, and buildings that you sometimes couldn't see the sky much, either.

Kate was dreamily loosing herself in the clear dome of sky when suddenly the cycle slowed and turned off the road. She blinked as she looked at a low wooden building and a sun-faded red sign that read OLDE WEST CURIOS.

"You want a curio?" she asked when the motor had sputtered off.

"Not likely. But doesn't this seem the sort of place where Pete would do business? If he's their supplier of Indian artifacts, he might have stopped, and we can find out if he got this far."

"You should go into police work," Kate said as she followed Jimmy toward the ramshackle building.

"Yeah, I know, like Charlie Chan."

Squinting in the dimness inside, they gradually made out counters and tables piled with merchandise. Bright

Indian baskets and silver belt buckles were stacked among ashtrays made from cow hooves. The walls were adorned with blankets and with pictures of cowboys and Indians painted on velvet. A bank of wooden shelves sagged beneath boxes of ore and rocks with crystals glinting under their coating of dust.

One corner of the store seemed devoted to Indian artifacts. Arrowheads and other stone tools filled boxes on several tables, while the more unusual items huddled in a dimly lit case.

"Can I help you?" Looking as dry and dusty as his shop, the proprietor stepped from a curtained-off back room.

"Oh, yeah, maybe," Jimmy began. "We're looking for a . . . for an acquaintance of ours. A guy named Pete. A big fellow, baldish, red beard. He deals in old Indian things, arrowheads and such."

"Potty Pete. He sure has got a lot of acquaintances. Just missed him, though. Left not half an hour ago. Checked on my supplies, said he'd stop with more his next time through. Indian stuff, you understand."

"Did he say where he was going?"

"Nope. Just headed west. But he's got a number of customers around. You might catch up with him."

"Thanks. We'll try." Jimmy was already replacing his helmet and heading out the door. "Maybe this Charlie Chan stuff isn't so bad," he said to Kate, once they were outside. "We're hot on the villain's trail."

"And we know he's called 'Potty Pete.' " She giggled. "I wonder if that's because he sells old pots or because he's potty in the head."

The air had lost all its morning coolness as they

95

continued west, and by their next stop Kate was more thrilled by the sign that advertised COLD DRINKS than by the one proclaiming ARROWHEADS, INDIAN CURIOS.

This establishment was more impressive than the last. Another sign, announcing it as INDIAN JACK'S TRADING POST, was freshly painted, and several cars were parked out front. None was a flame-streaked black van. The lights inside were brighter, too, and in one corner, slot machines flashed and clattered as one customer worked them methodically.

Behind the counter, a woman looked up as the bells over the door jangled. Her hair was pulled back in a loose gray knot, and her broad face, the color of warm sunbaked earth, was softened with a network of fine wrinkles. "Got some nice things here, kids," she said cheerily. "You like dolls?" she added, looking at Kate.

Kate frowned a little. She was much too old for dolls. Still, some of these were kind of special. She stepped up to the counter with the ranks and ranks of little figures.

"Eh, yeah. They're nice. Are they made around here?"

The woman leaned forward and said with a conspiratorial chuckle, "Well actually, the dolls, they're made in Taiwan. No good stuff really, pretty cheap. But the clothes, they're local. See." She picked up a little Indian woman swathed in a blue and red shawl and carrying a tiny basket on her back. "Women from all over the state make these clothes and things. They're different tribes—Shoshone, Paiute, Yokut, Ute. I like this one here, with the necklace. That's 'cause I'm Paiute, I guess, and anyway my cousin makes the jewelry."

Kate fingered the doll, tempted, but then she remembered her assignment. "Yes, it's very nice. I like it. But actually we're here looking for someone. Potty Pete. Has he been by this way?"

The woman's smiling, open face suddenly went blank. "I don't know. Got to check."

As the woman hurried into a back room, Kate smiled, a little surprised at herself. She'd been able to walk right up and talk to a stranger with hardly a qualm. Well, she had been a nice lady, and anyway it helped having a role to play: Special Investigator, Kate Elliot.

She'd joined Jimmy at a case full of cracked, old-looking pots, when the woman returned, all her jolliness put aside. "No, no, I'm sorry. Potty Pete's not been by this way, not for a long time. You look somewhere else, okay?"

"Oh, but . . ." Kate began.

"That's okay," Jimmy said firmly. "Guess we'll give up trying to find him. Thanks though." He hustled Kate out the jangling door.

"We're not giving up, are we?" Kate sputtered.

"Of course not. But I just looked out their side window. No, don't look around! There's more parking in back. And you know what's there?"

"A black van with red flames."

"Right. If Potty Pete's there, and the lady says he isn't, then he's on to the fact that we're following him. Someone's probably watching us right now."

Again Kate fought the urge to turn around. "So why don't we just march back in there and offer to buy the stone from him? That *is* his business."

"Well for one thing, he'd probably charge a fortune

for it. And besides, after last night, I kind of doubt he'd want to sell *me* anything. We haven't formed a real good business relationship."

"True. Well, so what do we do?"

"Get on our trusty steed and ride off as if we're giving up."

"Only to double back once we're out of sight?"

"You saw that movie, too."

"All of them."

Feeling as if guns were trained on them, the two mounted up and roared noisily onto the highway, heading back east. As soon as a dip in the road hid them from Indian Jack's, Jimmy turned off the highway and headed back across the dry unfenced land until they came to a gully.

Hiding the cycle in a clump of sage, they began hiking along the bottom of the gully as it sliced back toward the road. When they figured they were just north of the shop, they crawled up the dry weedy bank and lay like lizards peering over the rim. The van was still parked behind the building.

"Now what?" Kate whispered. The hot afternoon silence seemed to call for whispering, even though they were some distance from the building.

"Third time's the charm, I guess. The van's probably not locked now. Do you think you can pick out that stone from a bunch of others, if it's there, I mean?"

"Probably. By feel, if nothing else. I've been feeling it in my hand for a couple of weeks."

Crouching close to the ground, they scuttled forward, seeking whatever cover they could: sagebrush, a rusty abandoned car, a series of dilapidated outbuildings.

VISION QUEST

Finally they reached the shelter of a large shed built right against the side of the main building. They were just creeping past the half-open door towards the van, when Kate grabbed Jimmy's arm.

"I can hear voices. One sounds like Pete's."

They looked at each other, then slipped into the dim shed and made their way cautiously through saw-horses and piles of lumber to the far wall. Voices were rising and falling on the other side. Potty Pete's boom-ing bluster was unmistakable. Once they found spots clear of hanging hammers and ropes, each pressed an ear to the wall. Another, smaller voice was speaking.

". . . not the only supplier, of course, but your stuff is the best. Still, wouldn't it be less risky if you made fewer of the deliveries yourself? I mean, if you had a middleman."

"And you're applying for the job, aren't you, Jack? No, I'll keep control of deliveries, thanks. I'm good at it, and the boys at the town know it. Even the antiqui-ties people haven't caught on to me yet."

"All right, I won't push. But I'd like to do a little coming up in the world, too, you know. Anyway, are you guys so sure your ghost town is safe? What about stray tourists?"

"It's safe and you know it. Poor roads, on a forgotten patch of federal land, not on any of the maps or in the brochures. Your role is big enough, Jack. You're one of the few who knows where it is. Which means, inciden-tally, that if the authorities ever drop by, we'll have a pretty good idea of where they heard about us."

As Jack protested his loyalty, Jimmy whispered, "It sounds like he's the biggest illicit antiquities dealer around. He'll never miss one stone. Let's get to the van."

Kate nodded. She turned, and her eyes widened. Something moved across the open doorway; the rectangle of sunlight slowly shrank. And before either of them could stop it, the heavy plank door slammed. They heard a bolt slam shut. Footsteps receded into silence.

ELEVEN

"TERRIFIC," JIMMY MUTTERED. "NOW SOME TIDY door-closing type has locked us in here."

"Sure we weren't deliberately locked in?"

"Why? If we'd been seen, we'd have been dragged out for Potty Pete to manhandle. Besides"—he lowered his voice even further—"you can still hear him next door."

"Well, let's see if we can break out of here. It's a toolshed, after all."

They felt around and finally located a file with which they quietly tried to pry off the door hinges. Nothing gave. Then they worked around the shed, feeling for loose planks. Again, no results.

"We could always start banging and screaming and making a fuss," Kate suggested halfheartedly.

"Go ahead, I can't wait to hear you explain how we happen to be here."

"Well, then . . ."

"Hush!"

At the other end of the shed, there was the sound of the lock being opened. The door creaked ajar, showing a pale strip of evening light. Before the two had finished

101

crouching down, something thumped on the shed floor, and abruptly the door was closed and locked, again.

After a moment Kate and Jimmy crept toward the thing. "A bomb, maybe?" Kate suggested, as Jimmy reached for the white lump.

"It's not ticking. Feels more like a plastic bag full of . . . hmm." He reached inside. "It is! Potato chips, a couple of soft drinks, two candy bars."

"Rations," Kate said glumly. "We definitely are prisoners."

"There's also a piece of paper, a note." He held the square of white up to a knothole. "Not much light left. It says . . . yeah. 'If you value your lives, don't leave the shed until I let you out.' "

"Pretty melodramatic."

"Yeah, and maybe a good idea, too."

"You think so?"

"Well, I don't hear voices next door anymore. We'd probably break out of here just in time to run into Pete. I really don't want to get caught breaking into his van again."

"So you just want us to stay here like rats in a trap?"

"Hey, I don't exactly *want* it!" Jimmy snapped. "Come on, let's eat. Maybe our brains will be recharged, and we'll think of something."

Before they'd finished eating, however, they heard footsteps, the slam of a car door, and an engine starting up. Kate jumped up and put her eye to the knothole. At first she saw nothing, then a black van passed through her small circle of sight.

"He's going, he's getting away! What'll we do?"

"Not much, by the looks of it."

A long, glum silence was broken by a voice, low and muffled, coming through the planks of the locked door. "You kids, listen to me. You stay in there till morning. You try to get out before then, and I blow your heads off. Understand?"

The footsteps moved away without the person waiting for a reply, but there wasn't much to say. It seemed they were spending a long night in this shed. Kate leaned back against a coil of rope. There was no way she could sleep. She was too angry—and frightened.

At first, the anger was aimed at herself, then it moved to whomever had locked them in. And that was where the fear came from, too. What sort of crime syndicate had they stumbled onto? All she wanted was to get one carved stone and put it where it belonged. And look where it'd gotten her!

There, you see, she told herself. That's what comes of getting tied up with people, past or present. Just like her father. In the darkness, her thoughts drifted toward him. She wondered if he'd regretted it, in his barracks at night, knowing that the next day or the next he might get killed trying to help people he thought needed him. Maybe, but knowing him, that probably wouldn't have stopped him. She shook her head, trying to hug her resentment to her, but in the end she felt only sadness. Her own and its ancient echo.

The chinks between the wallboards were again faintly gray when the door rattled and swung open. Befuddled a moment, Kate sat up, blinking at the dark figure silhouetted in the doorway. She heard Jimmy stirring from his nest under the sawhorses.

"Okay, you kids, come over here." The voice did not sound as muffled or as menacing as before. Staggering to their feet, the two walked to the doorway. Slowly the figure folded up and sat on the ground just outside. "Sit down, you two; we need to talk."

Kate squinted. It was the woman at the shop counter, the one who'd said Pete wasn't there when he was.

She and Jimmy exchanged doubtful glances, then they shrugged and sat just inside the door.

"Now," the woman began, "I want to know why you two are chasing Potty Pete all over the countryside. He said that you, boy, tried to break into his van twice. Were you planning that a third time? That's like playing with fire, you know."

"We need something he has," Jimmy said simply.

"Well maybe you do, maybe you don't. I won't lecture you. But you sure don't need it bad enough to get killed for it. Pete may not be the biggest criminal in the state, but he's no petty crook. He takes himself real seriously."

Kate spoke up. "We're really not concerned about the law or any of that. Of course he shouldn't be doing what he does, but we're not on a crusade to stop him. It's just that he has one stone that we need. We have to get it back . . . to its owner. We'd even buy it, if he gave us a chance."

"A stone?"

"Yes, a carved charm stone. Smooth black with a spiral groove. He didn't sell it to you, did he?"

The woman almost seemed to chuckle. "No, we didn't buy anything like that. But what's so important about an old stone?"

Jimmy answered. "Like Kate said, we've got to return it someplace. But hey, you're the one who's the Indian. It's your heritage Pete's messing around with. Digging up your ancestors' sacred things and all."

"They're not my ancestors. I'm Paiute. The old ones were something else. But if you think my being Indian should make it important to me, how come it is to you? You two don't exactly look one hundred percent Indian."

"But we *are* people," Jimmy protested. "So it's our heritage, too."

The woman sighed. "Okay, I'm people, too. I care about heritage. My grandma used to make baskets and tell me stories, just like the old people who made those stones, I bet. My grandma loved kids, I love kids, and those old people probably did, too. And they wouldn't, any of them, want young kids getting mixed up with wicked folks who'd as soon kill them as say hello.

"Maybe I don't like what Pete does, but it's tied up in my life and I can't stop that. But I can lock up a couple of kids to keep them from getting killed. My grandma would have done that, and so would the old ones, I bet. That's the kind of heritage I care about."

Kate was trying not to like this woman, but it was getting hard. "You did threaten to blow our heads off."

The woman nodded, smiling slowly. "They say that on TV a lot. Worked pretty good, huh?"

Jimmy stood up. "I don't suppose you'd tell us which way Pete headed last night?"

The woman just kept smiling.

"So, we're free to go?" Kate asked.

"It's a free country." Slowly the woman stood up and stepped out of the doorway. "Just don't go chasing around it after stuff that's not important."

Dawn was smearing across the eastern horizon as Kate and Jimmy trudged back along the gully to where they'd hidden the cycle. Watching the gold fade into blue, they sat largely in silence, eating a makeshift breakfast.

At last Kate stood up and looked toward the road. "Well, we've got three choices, I guess: back to Argentum, on to Tanner River, or try to find Pete again."

"Kate," Jimmy said as he screwed the lid back on his canteen, "I hate to point this out, but Nevada's a big state. Potty Pete the mad pothunter could be about anywhere in it by now."

"True, but remember what that other guy said, something about Pete operating out of a ghost town. We could try to find it. That's probably where all the antiquities are stored."

"Yeah, but there are about as many ghost towns in this state as there are rattlesnakes. And Pete even said that this one wasn't on the maps or in the guides. We told our folks we'd be gone three or four days. It would take us months to check out all the ghost towns." He stood up. "Blast that lady, anyway. She sure fouled things up!"

"She didn't mean to."

"I know, but she did. And she was wrong about stones, too. I mean, sure it's people that are important, but stones can help you learn about people."

"And help them," Kate muttered, then wished she hadn't. Yet, though she hated to admit it, she did want to help Wadat and Hizu. And it wasn't just to make them leave her alone—not anymore. She'd come to care about them. Automatically, she clenched her fists, then relaxed. Well, she wouldn't make a habit of it. She could go back to being a safe little island after this was all over.

As if picking up her thoughts, Jimmy asked, "Hey, have you been seeing those lights lately?"

She thought a moment. "No, I haven't, not since we left Argentum. Maybe that's because I'm at least *trying* to do something."

"Well, then, we'd better keep it up." Jimmy rolled the cycle out of the shrubs. "I think Tanner River's not too far from here, though it's off to the south. We might as well go there and at least accomplish *something* we set out to do."

With a resigned sigh, Kate rammed on her helmet. "All right. Let's go."

Consulting a map, they traced what looked like a fairly direct route. On the ground, however, most of it proved to be a rutted dirt road which sometimes faded out altogether. Progress was slow, and a dramatic crimson sunset found them still several miles from their goal.

Jimmy pulled to a stop on a small rise. He pointed to hills darkening against a boiling sky. "See that little knob jutting out beyond that other hill? That's where the petroglyphs are. The river's on the far side along that line of trees. It must've been a great hunting spot. Migrating deer would be forced by the bend in the river to go right between that outcrop and the other slope. If the Indians put barricades in the right spots, they could've made quite a haul."

Kate looked at the distant hill, dark and hunched against a bloody sky. "Are we going to spend the night there?"

"We could. But it's so dark, we really should camp here and head there first thing in the morning."

"Good." The thought of spending the night among more ancient petroglyphs suddenly had no appeal.

Too tired to cook, they ate corned beef and peaches straight from cans. Before they crawled into their sleeping bags, Jimmy took a coil of rope and spread it on the ground encircling their little camp.

"What's that for?" Kate asked. "Just being tidy?"

"It's supposed to keep snakes out. They like to slither into cuddly warm sleeping bags, you know."

Kate shuddered. "That's not barrier enough to keep anything out."

"Well, supposedly snakes don't like crawling over coarse hemp rope. Guess it scratches their bellies. It's probably just an old wives' tale, but the cowboys always used to do it."

Kate crawled into her bag and pulled the drawstring very tight. She envisioned waking in the morning to find seething masses of frustrated snakes waiting outside the rope.

After a minute, Jimmy spoke from the darkness.

VISION QUEST

"You know, Kate, when we first ran into Pete at that camp, I thought it was pretty terrific luck. But then I began thinking that it was all a bit much for coincidence, that maybe these spirits we're dealing with had somehow taken a hand."

Kate was startled at how his thoughts were echoing her own. "And now what do you think?"

He chuckled. "Well, there're spirits and spirits, I guess. Lots of Indian tribes had a trickster spirit, a coyote. He liked to cause trouble and lead folks astray. I guess that's why they needed a shaman. Dealing with spirits isn't easy."

With only her face exposed to the cold desert air, Kate looked up into the sky, glittering each moment with more and more stars. A meteor broke loose and arched down to the horizon. Spirits may not be easy to deal with, but it was certainly easy to think about them in a place like this. No clutter, no phoniness, the world unchanged since its beginning. Somewhere a coyote raised a high, yapping song. Out of a cold distance, another answered.

Tricksters? Maybe, but still part of things here. That's what Wadat and Hizu had been, part of the land and its ways. Her own people didn't share that, and Kate wasn't sure she wanted to, not fully. She certainly hadn't wanted these visions, she thought sleepily. She just wasn't cut out to be a shaman.

What came to her then was not really a vision. It was a dream. But it was not her dream.

He dreamed he was dressed in his shaman regalia, with the deer skin hanging down his back and the antlered skull perched heavily on his head. He stood waiting behind the rock where the spirits had told him to stand, waiting for the first hunt of this reluctant new shaman. Hidden around him crouched the hunters in places the vision had shown they should be. He had performed all the rituals as Hizu had taught him, and he hoped he had interpreted the vision aright. Yet he knew that around him where there should be faith and confidence, fear and doubt lay as thick as smoke.

Wadat was the only shaman they had, the only one who knew the rituals. Only he could direct the hunt. But still, he could feel them thinking, he was a mere child and one taught by Hizu, the forgotten. Might he not fail them, too, as his teacher had done? From where the hunters and beaters lay hidden, their thoughts rose in a choking cloud. He felt dizzy with fear.

A clear birdcall cut the afternoon stillness. The lookout had spotted deer. Soon now, soon. But it was not soon; he seemed to wait there forever. The deer-hoof rattle hung silent and heavy in one hand. With the other he touched the comforting stone that pressed against the side of his medicine bag.

Then he saw them, deer coming this way. They were nervous and skittish, perhaps sensing a trap. Had he placed the barriers in the right spots? The vision had been blurry and difficult to read. There were more deer now and more. The beaters jumped out of hiding, shouting and waving sticks, driving the deer forward. The panicked herd bolted his way. All exactly as it should be.

No, not exactly. Not at all! One buck leaped a brush

fence, then another. The fences were too low and not in the perfect spots, he could see that now. But too late! Deer after deer turned aside, escaping before they were in reach of the bowmen.

The archers leaped out and chased the fleeing deer, but it was too late. The hunt had failed; he had failed! He had failed Hizu, and now he had failed his people. Surely now they would cast his body on the rocks, scatter his soul to the wind. Like Hizu, he would wander forever, lost, never to be a part of the land. The hunters turned. They were coming for him even now.

Wadat sat up screaming, clutching his rabbit-skin blanket around him. Dawn was reddening the sky, silhouetting the dark humped hill where the hunt would be. The hunt was yet to come. This had been only a dream.

But it was a true dream, he knew it. It would all happen just as he had seen it. He was doomed.

Shaking in fear, he called out, "Spirit of the soaring eagle, spirits of earth and air and water. Help me! Please help me! I am so alone!"

Wildly he sang the chant of the eagle spirit. But the haunting tune trailed off in surprise. There was someone sitting near him on the ground. She huddled in wrappings like another suddenly awakened sleeper. He looked into her eyes. They were wide and blue as the eagle's vast sky.

TWELVE

"KATE?" JIMMY SAID SLEEPILY, "DID YOU SCREAM, or was it another coyote?"

"Somebody screamed," she said from where she sat clutching her sleeping bag around her. "It might have been me."

Jimmy sat up, looking like a plump green caterpillar in his bag. "Dreams?"

She nodded.

"Bad ones?"

"Yes. Very bad, very old." She didn't want to say anymore. If he hadn't shared the dream, he'd been lucky.

"Well," Jimmy said after a moment, "the sun's up. Time we were, too."

They breakfasted largely in silence. Kate still felt the dream hanging over her, a cloud heavy with doom. But as the sun rose higher above the eastern peaks, the cloud thinned a little, like morning mist.

She was brushing her hair into its ponytail, when a sharp cry drew her eyes upward. "Look!" she said, standing up. "An eagle, I think."

VISION QUEST

Jimmy grabbed for his pair of binoculars and trained it on the bird. "That's one huge bird, all right. Probably it's an eagle. I don't . . . Would you look at that!"

"What?"

"Look lower, at the base of those hills."

A plume of dust was rising along a road that fringed a tumbled range of hills. As they watched, it turned and headed up an even fainter track that cut into a tree-scattered canyon.

Silently Jimmy handed her the binoculars. In a moment she'd found the dust plume and its source: a black van streaked with red flames.

"Those old spirits again," Jimmy said, only half laughing as he struggled to flatten out a map. "Look, the map shows those hills are federal land. There's even a mark for an old mine, though nothing for a ghost town."

As Jimmy folded the map, Kate looked at him. "Do we go?"

"It's what they want us to do, isn't it?" This time he was serious.

"The spirits?"

He didn't answer, and Kate knew he was afraid to put too much into words, just as she was.

"All right," she said, walking to the motorcycle. "Let's just hope that this time it's eagles, not coyotes."

There was no road between their camp and the distant track, but the ground was firm and not rutted, better than some of the roads they had used. Before long, their cycle brought them to where the van had disappeared. Anxiously they followed a tire-marked road up into the hills.

VISION QUEST

Already the cool morning shadows had shortened, and a hot wind was blowing down the little canyon. Sage and pinyon pine scarcely clothed the rocky slopes, and an occasional startled jackrabbit bounded ahead.

Where the road skirted a large mound of gravelly earth, Jimmy pulled the cycle over. "That's one of the old mine tailings. We must be getting near the ghost town. Better hide the bike and walk."

Once the cycle was concealed, the two crept up the road, keeping an eye open for snakes and signs of an abandoned town.

"I've never seen a real ghost town," Kate said after awhile, "except for Virginia City, of course."

"That tourist trap? Virginia City's no ghost town. It's much too hokey for any ghost to be caught dead in." He laughed softly. "I like that, no ghost would be . . ."

Kate silenced him by pointing ahead. "Aren't those buildings up there through the trees?"

He stared. "Yeah, looks like it. Well, we can't just walk into town like in some Western shoot-out. Let's cut off through the trees and come at it from the side. Then maybe we can scout the place out and see where they keep their loot."

The trees near the town were fairly dense, dark juniper mixed with scraggly pinyon pine. The wind fretted through their branches with a dry rattling. The two worked their way up the canyon until they guessed they were about level with the buildings they'd seen from the road.

They were about to turn in that direction, when Kate saw stones sticking up through the brush in a

clearing. "Are those foundations for more buildings?"
They walked closer. "No," Jimmy said after a moment. "Looks like we've found the town cemetery."

Kate tensed, then told herself not to be a superstitious twit. She could see now that they were standing among a cluster of low earth mounds. Some were marked with white marble headstones, others with rough planks, their painted inscriptions long ago weathered off. Many of the stones were cracked and broken, but some of the writing could still be read.

"Boy, here's someone who really lived a long time," Jimmy whispered. " 'Gertrude Patricia Culver, seventeen seventy-eight to eighteen seventy-three.' That makes her . . . eh, ninety-five. And look at this one. 'Horace Polyphemus Philpot.' What a name!"

Kate was looking instead at a low white stone, carved like a sleeping lamb. " 'Sarah Ann McKelvey'," she read. " 'Eighteen sixty-seven to eighteen seventy-two.' Oh, how sad. She was only five."

"My sister Susie's just five now," Jimmy said, then was silent for a moment. "Good thing we have better medicine these days. Come on, it's kind of spooky here. Let's get going."

As they carefully stepped over the little weed-covered mounds, Kate wondered about Jimmy's family. His ancestors had apparently been in Argentum for over a century. Uncle Bernie said that a lot of Chinese had been brought in during the silver years to work the mines and do menial jobs.

"What about Chinese?" she asked. "Do you suppose any lived in this town and were buried here?"

Jimmy snorted. "Not here. Over there maybe, beyond that little rusty fence. The good Christian folk didn't let Chinese into their graveyards. They had to be buried outside."

"That's awful!"

"Yeah, but things have changed, officially at least. Now the good folks of Argentum would probably let me get buried in their little cemetery—if I can't find someplace better to die."

Kate shuddered. "Well, let's be careful and not put it to the test for a while."

Through a screen of trees, they could now see the ghost town itself. It stretched for a couple of blocks along a weedy dirt road. Some of the buildings had collapsed into heaps of lumber; others slumped to one side or sagged in the middle like swaybacked horses. A few, though equally weathered and gray, stood upright and even had glass in some of their windows.

This place had been abandoned for years and years, Kate thought, yet it still had a raw, naked look. Back East, an empty building was lost under vines and weeds in no time. Uncle Bernie had said something about how in the West, man's scars on the land were fewer, but they took longer to heal. And here you could certainly see that.

Jimmy pointed to one of the more intact buildings, one with a couple of cars and the black van parked out front. "Let's hope that if they live in there, they store their artifacts someplace else. I don't want to sneak that charm stone out from under Pete's bed."

"So let's case the joint."

Using the ruined buildings as cover, they slipped

closer to those still standing. But they had to move carefully. The ground behind the buildings was strewn with old junk: rusty barrel hoops, tin cans, old bedsprings, parts of an ornate metal stove.

They had reached the far end of town and were about to pelt across the street, when a man stepped out of one of the buildings. "Down!" Jimmy warned, but Kate had already flattened herself behind a tuft of high yellow grass.

The man was thinner and darker than Pete. He opened the back doors of the van, rummaged a moment, then pulled out a big cardboard box. He took this into another building, where the faded sign proclaimed EMILE JOHNSTON, GENERAL MERCHANDISE. He repeated this with several more boxes, and finally Pete came out of the first building. The two talked a moment, then both went back inside.

"Looks like that old store's what we want," Jimmy whispered. "Too bad it's next to Pete's. We'll have to be very sneaky."

"Sneaky's my middle name."

They crept further up the street, and when a bend hid them from the main buildings, they dashed across. Stealthily they began working back toward their target.

"Sure this is the right one?" Kate whispered as they crouched beneath a back window. "I've sort of lost track."

"Yes, it's got the same sickly green paint. Let's try this other window, most of the glass is out. I think we can just squeeze through."

They did, barely. Kate crawled through headfirst. She hated putting her hands to the floor, convinced that awful dead things might be lying there. But all she encountered was dust.

She got up and looked back out through one of the remaining glass panes. Wavy and full of bubbles, it was like looking through water. Then she studied the gloomy interior. Some sort of storeroom. Dusty crates were piled along the walls. She peeked into one and found piles of yellowed paper chewed into cozy mouse nests. Behind the crates, various patterns of wallpaper were peeling in strips off the walls. Not much here. Jimmy was already creaking open the door into the next room.

It was a big room and long, stretching all the way to the display windows up front. The air smelled dead and musty. Shelves ran the length of both walls, and in the light from the dust-filmed windows, they could make out a large front counter.

Cautiously they walked forward. Bulky shapes slowly became recognizable as their eyes adjusted to the gloom. A tipped-over wooden keg had spilled a rusty avalanche of nails, and the merchandise that had once covered the shelves had been pushed in heaps onto the floor. Kate glimpsed old tins of baking powder and tobacco, a coffee mill, stacks of chipped enamel bowls, and a metal tangle she finally recognized as a bird cage.

Replacing these on most of the shelves were new cardboard boxes labeled with scrawled black markers. Squinting at one, she saw it said CHACO POTTERY, BLACK ON WHITE. BIRD HEADS AND EFFIGY POTS read the one beside it.

"This is the place, all right," Kate whispered.

"Sure is," Jimmy said longingly as he peeked into a

box he'd opened. He pulled out a long leaf-shaped blade, its faceted black surface catching even the dull light. "They must have a fortune in looted stuff here. Wherever are we going to start looking for that one charm stone? If it's even here and not still in the van or sold to someone along the way."

"Let's try the boxes on the counter. They must be the ones the man just brought in, or at least they've been put here recently."

Kate looked at the stacks of boxes and unfolded the flaps of one. Lumps were wrapped in wadded-up newspaper. It could take days to systematically check through each one of these boxes, she thought gloomily. Yet her empty right hand seemed to be closed around the weight of that still-missing stone. Where was it?

She stepped back. Obviously there was no time to develop a system. Half closing her eyes, she surveyed the boxes. She stopped at one, second from the top of its pile. The design on the cardboard side proclaimed that it had once carried SUN BRAND ORANGES.

After struggling to move the top box, she ripped into the second. Eagerly she felt through the wrapped-up stones. One slipped into her hand, fitting as if it had always been there. Tingling with awe, she pulled it out. Smooth and black, a single groove spiraled down its tapered length.

"I've got it!" she said firmly.

Jimmy raised his head from the box he'd been pawing through. "How could you . . . Look out, someone's coming." Still staring out the window, he crouched behind the counter. "Sure you've got the right stone?"

119

"Yes."

"Then let's go."

Like rats, they scuttled for the back of the store just as the front door opened.

"Sure, we've a great bunch of stuff here," a voice said. Pete's, Kate realized. "But we've got to put together a better selection for the road. If I carried a wider price range, I'd break into more markets."

"If you don't watch out, Pete, you'll blow our cover."

"Hey, this stuff makes good money on its own. Don't knock it. And the only expense is the gas for driving around and digging up old sites."

"Yeah, I know, every bit counts. But your part's frosting, Pete, and you know it."

"Frosting's the best part; anyone knows that."

"Aren't we witty, though? Well, we knew you weren't cut out for farming when we started. Go ahead, put together your own batch. Jeff said his load won't be ready for a couple of days anyway."

As the two men talked in the front of the store, Kate and Jimmy were creeping toward the back. They'd almost reached the storeroom door when Kate heard Jimmy squeak. Seconds later a rake handle clattered to the floor. In panic, Jimmy lunged for the door with Kate right after him.

"What was that? Hey, there's someone back there!" Footsteps running heavily through the store.

Jimmy, then Kate dove through the back window. They tumbled over each other, then leaped up. The spindly pine trees looked as if they'd make pretty poor cover.

VISION QUEST

"In here!" Kate hissed as she sprinted for the small sagging house next door. They pushed open the back door and ran through the kitchen. Kate had a fleeting glimpse of a rusty stove and gaping cupboard doors before they were in a bedroom.

A cracked mirror gleamed dully on the wall, and a painted metal bedstead still stood in the center of the room, supporting a mouse-chewed mattress.

Jimmy dropped to his stomach and slid under the bed. Kate held back, then, hearing voices outside, she reluctantly followed. All manner of dead and ghastly things could be under there. She tried to curl up as tight as a sow bug and touch as little as possible.

"You go that way, I'll go this." Pete's voice.

"Probably just some curious hikers."

"We can't risk it. Got to find them."

Footsteps outside. Then silence. Then footsteps coming in through the front of the house.

"Anyone in here? Come on out!" Boots tromping right by the bed. "What a dump. Why couldn't I find a nice clean office job?"

The boots clumped out through the kitchen and the back door. The silence stretched on and on. Kate could hear only her breathing and Jimmy's next to her. She couldn't see a thing except a bed leg and something white near it. Bored, she focused on that. Something white and roundish. Dents on one side.

She almost screamed. A skull! Whimpering, she shuffled farther back.

"Quiet!" Jimmy whispered. "Give them time to get farther away."

121

Silent with horror, she stared at the hideous thing not a foot from her face. A small skull. Its eyes were open, staring at her. Shouldn't it have eye sockets instead of eyes? After all those years surely . . . Terror dwindled into relief.

A doll's head. A china doll, cracked and hairless, kicked under the bed. She thought of Sarah Ann McKelvey, aged five, lying in the graveyard. Relief turned to sadness.

"Couldn't we go now?" she whispered.

"Yeah, let's. Someone less tidy might check back here."

They wriggled from under the bed, stirring up clouds of dust. Halfheartedly they brushed at their clothes as they tiptoed to the back door.

Nothing moved outside. Silently they slipped out the door, then flitted like ghosts behind the dilapidated buildings until they reached the end of town. The street was deserted except for one lone tumbleweed and a spiraling dust devil. Together Kate and Jimmy sprinted across.

They'd almost reached the cover of an old barn when they heard a shout. "Up there!"

Jimmy ducked through the barn door. Strips of light showed between the wallboards. Bundles of dried leaves hung from the rafters and were stacked in bales along one wall. Kate thought it smelled sweet and green, hay maybe.

"We could hide behind those," she called, running toward the bales.

"No, let's . . ."

VISION QUEST

The floorboards creaked and snapped. Kate was falling. Wildly she flailed at floor beams and Jimmy's outstretched arm. She grabbed him just as other boards gave way, and both tumbled down into darkness.

Over their own startled squeals, they heard other voices. "There! In the barn!"

THIRTEEN

KATE SAT ON SOMETHING SOFT, DRY, AND CRACK-ling. The smell was sweet and minty.

"Still in one piece?" said a shaky voice beside her.

"I think so."

"Good. Head for that door."

Crawling toward a low, light-fringed hatch, Kate soon scrambled after Jimmy into the sunlight. Voices from the front of the barn were calling, "Where?" "They fell through!"

"Look out, you ass, it's all rotten. Ladder's over there."

More voices came from farther down the street, but they all dropped quickly behind as Kate and Jimmy pelted down the steep slope beyond the barn. Spiky branches reached out at them, but they ducked and twisted aside. Birds twittered out of their way as they skidded over pebbly dirt and slippery pine needles.

At the bottom of the slope, the two found themselves in a side valley that forked off from the one they had traveled up earlier. They charged through a field of waving shoulder-high stalks. The thin purple-green leaves had jagged-looking edges, but felt velvety soft as

VISION QUEST

Kate brushed past them, stirring up the sweet minty smell.

A sharp crack split the air. Gunshot! A cloud of squawking crows rose from the trees. Another shot.

"Kate," Jimmy yelled, "we're in big trouble!"

"Brilliant deduction, Charlie Chan."

"No, I mean *big* trouble."

"Just run; the bike can't be far."

It wasn't. No sooner had they cleared the field than they burst through a screen of pines onto the dirt road. Not far away were the tailings where they'd hidden the motorcycle. There were no parting shots, but the two didn't need them to speed their departure.

Once on the cycle, they raced downhill like daredevil stuntmen until they were well out of the ghost town's canyon and bouncing over open country. The petroglyph hill rose small and dark in the distance. By then Kate had calmed down and noticed that some of their gear was coming loose.

Jimmy had seen it, too, and slowed to a stop. "Better tighten these straps," he said. "We can't afford to lose our stuff way out here."

Kate got off and walked around, gratefully stretching her legs. Jimmy discovered a broken strap and tried to tighten their gear without it. Both of her pockets felt heavy with stones. She reached in and touched them, both solid and real. What an incredible relief to have them both! These last couple of days had been like some absurd movie. But now all they had to do was find where to bury Hizu's stone, and this craziness would be over.

She'd started poking in a bag for some food when

Jimmy said, "No time for a break. Soon as I fix this, we've got to move. They might follow us."

"Oh, come on, that's over. All we did was steal one stone that they'll never miss. We could've been a couple of hikers exploring a ghost town."

"Maybe you didn't notice them shooting at us?"

"That was just to scare us off. They wouldn't want to really kill us."

"Oh? We know where their hideout is and what they're doing there."

"Ah, I know this is the wild West, but no one would murder a couple of kids just to keep a stolen artifact business quiet."

"I thought you city girls knew all about this sort of thing."

"What sort of thing?"

"Pot. That stuff in the barn and growing in the field. It's marijuana. I just figured it out. They're using their artifact peddling as a cover and a way to make contact with folks who're willing to deal in even more illegal things. They could have stuff besides pot going, too."

"Oh." The relief she'd been feeling vanished. They *were* in trouble, in a whole different league of trouble. But suddenly a lot of things made sense. "That's why the woman at the curio shop wanted to protect us from Pete, and why she thought it was so funny that we were only after an old stone."

"Potty Pete," Jimmy chuckled. "The nickname's not for pot hunting *or* nuttiness."

"What a couple of innocents we are."

Jimmy gave the rope he had used to tighten the pack

a last pull and swung onto the cycle. "We may be dumb, but we're not dead. Not yet. Let's go!"

Kate was just climbing on behind him when she noticed a thin column of dust on the distant road. She pointed. "You saw that?"

"Yes. Move it!"

They shot off in a spray of gravel. Kate looked behind at their distant pursuers, then yelled ahead to Jimmy, "They'll have a harder time than we will, cutting across country in that van."

Jimmy nodded and concentrated on avoiding ruts, rocks, and clumps of sage.

Kate kept looking between the dark hill ahead and the wisp of dust behind. The hill didn't seem to be growing bigger nearly fast enough, though what sanctuary it could offer, she wasn't sure. At least there'd be better places to hide, more than on this lunar plain anyway.

Often the pursuing vehicle dropped from sight behind dips in the ground. But always it reappeared and seemed closer each time. Kate wondered how that awkward van could do so well over this ground. Then she began to see. The growing blob under the dust cloud was not black. It was more a dirty green.

She leaned forward. "Bad news. I think they're using a jeep, not the van." Jimmy only growled and kept his eyes forward.

They were nearing Tanner River. Ahead, its tree-fringed bank swung by the base of a rocky hill. Between willows and cottonwoods, Kate caught a glimpse of water, water the color of coffee with a lot of milk. Over

127

their own whining engine, she could hear the steady rush of the river. Then another sound, the sharp twang of gunfire.

Terrified, Kate swiveled around. The jeep was much closer; she could clearly see the two men riding in it. She couldn't believe this sort of thing happened in real life. But the bullets seemed very real.

Jimmy poured on all the speed he could, skimming along the bending river, keeping clear of the soft grassy bank. Afraid to turn around, Kate kept her eyes on the rocky hill, looming at last on their left. Just beyond it, she could see a sloping saddle, a low pass between the hill and a steep mountain beyond. She couldn't be sure, but animals seemed to be moving along the saddle. Cattle? No, the color was too light. Deer maybe, or antelope. They'd scatter soon enough when this caval-cade burst upon them.

Kate glanced behind, but the jeep was hidden behind a shoulder of the hill. Jimmy turned them abruptly from the river and began climbing into the boulder-strewn pass. Better cover here.

Also, lots of deer, a whole herd of them. The air was dusty, so she couldn't see them too well. But they were there, daintily picking their way up the pass, not flinch-ing at the sight of the roaring motorcycle.

Suddenly Jimmy swerved. He'd barely missed one. Kate watched the animal as they swept past it. It didn't even turn its head.

A shiver ran through her. These deer weren't here at all, not now at least. Hundreds of years ago they had trotted up this quiet waiting pass. She remembered her dream, Wadat's dream. Her stomach churned.

Again she looked behind. She could see the jeep now, much closer. It was swerving wildly through an oblivious patch of ghostly deer. Whatever force was at work here was very strong. It had to be if it was reaching out to the men in the jeep as well as to Jimmy and her.

Another gunshot. Kate wondered whether they or the deer were the target. A ping on a nearby rock answered her question. She huddled down trying to make herself very small.

The shadowy deer were everywhere now, and suddenly they were running. Misty, sparsely clad men had leaped out at them, waving branches and driving them toward a low fence of brush. Some deer started to swerve, but then others leaped over and through it, escaping the men.

The slope was steep, and the cycle slowed to a nightmare crawl. Desperately Jimmy gunned the engine, aiming for a concealing cluster of boulders.

Ahead, one huge rock stood out from the rest. It's surface blazed with a spiral sun-sign. The sight cut through Kate like a bolt of lightning. And suddenly the whole hillside trembled and changed. Vision became reality.

The deer were no longer shadowy, no longer rushing past in unseeing waves. They were solid and real. A panicky herd of warm-smelling hides, jabbing antlers, white fear-gleaming eyes. The air was choked with dust and throbbing with the shouts of now-real hunters.

The cycle swerved wildly. It was bearing down on a

weak point in the fence and the deer escaping through it. A frightened buck charged right in front of them. Jimmy jammed his hand on the horn.

The buck bounded aside as the engine screeched, and the cycle skidded into the fence. Like a wave hitting rock, the fleeing wide-eyed deer swerved away from the noisy horror that had suddenly appeared in their midst. They charged up the hillside toward the rocks where the hunters hid, toward a volley of arrows.

Behind them, came other yelling voices and the angry blast of a car horn. Stumbling off the sprawling cycle, Kate looked around. The jeep, too, had been brought into this time. It was caught in a sea of real deer, hunters, and flying arrows. The second man screamed and grabbed at an arrow quivering in his arm.

Pete snarled something at him, then pointed ahead toward Jimmy and Kate. He leaped from the jeep, gun raised.

Abandoning their cycle, the two charged up the hill toward the nearest boulders. Kate felt panic driving her legs forward. Gunshot twanged beside her. Would she ever reach that first rock?

A sudden howling cry, and a nightmare figure leaped from behind the rock. It walked upright but had the great antlered head of a deer. It wailed and jibbered like a lost soul, then with a menacing snarl it sprang forward. The air shivered with a great dry rattling.

Kate stared, then remembered the gun and dove with Jimmy behind the rock. They huddled in its shadow, gasping for breath. No more gunshot, but over the eerie wailing, voices cried in fear. Moments later an engine roared, then gradually faded under the sounds of the hunt.

When Jimmy and Kate finally peered around the rock, the jeep was only a distant column of dust, which suddenly shimmered and faded into unreality. Some of the hunters stood, staring in awe at where it had been. Others turned that look on their young shaman. Several older men walked up to him, spoke a few pleased words, then joined the others.

Time passed. Men, women, and children ranged over the pass, retrieving arrows or butchering deer on the spot. Wealth lay all about them, enough meat and hides to secure life for a long while.

Only Wadal stood apart. Wearily he took off the heavy deer headdress and put it on the ground. Then he turned toward the lone rock where Kate and Jimmy stood silent in the shadow.

Slowly Kate reached into her pocket and pulled out the black spiral-carved stone. She held it forward into the light.

The boy looked at it for a long moment. A smile trembled on his lips, and Kate saw tears blur his eyes and run down his scarred cheek.

An ache deep inside her flared, then slowly began to fade. Her own eyes blurred with tears. And when she wiped them away, there was nothing to see. The boy was gone. The hillside was bare. No hunters, no deer. Not even the flutter of carrion crows. Only the hot afternoon silence.

Legs suddenly weak, Kate sat down at the base of the

rock. Jimmy did the same. For minutes they said nothing. A dry wind ruffled the stillness.

"Kate," Jimmy said finally, "I really don't think I'm up to visions—or whatever. But you never told me about that last dream. Did it come true?"

"It wasn't really my dream. It was his. But no, it didn't come true. Not all of it." She turned and looked at Jimmy. "But it would have, if we hadn't been there."

"You mean if we hadn't frightened the deer and turned them back into the arrows."

"Yes. Otherwise his first hunt would have failed. And a failed shaman . . ."

Jimmy nodded. "It was a fair exchange, then."

She looked at him questioningly.

"Well, Pete and the other guy were probably pretty freaked out by the hunt, but the weird shaman must've been the last straw. If he hadn't appeared just then, we'd have been shot full of holes and left for the buzzards."

Kate shuddered, but to her surprise, Jimmy began to laugh. "At least those two didn't lose out totally. They'll have quite a story to tell."

"Not a soul will believe them."

"Ah, but they do have an arrowhead souvenir in that fellow's arm."

"A fair exchange for the charm stone, then." She looked down at the stone lying dark and heavy in her hand. "But this really only belongs in one place."

Getting onto her knees, she began scrabbling at the dirt and rock beneath the petroglyph-marked boulder. Jimmy joined her.

VISION QUEST

When the hole seemed deep enough, Kate reached into it, opened her fingers, and let the cool, smooth stone slip from them. Her hand felt light and free.

In silence the two filled in the hole, patting the dirt and gravel until the spot looked no different from any other patch of earth.

A dry wind blew down from the hillside, carrying a wisp of tune, old and welcoming. Then in a swirl of dust, it blew away.

FOURTEEN

THE WIND IN THE GULLY WAS HOT AND DRY. IT smelled of sage and pine. It smelled of home.

With each upward step, Kate admired the patterns of light and shadow, the colors of the sun-glinting stones underfoot. This was the sort of land one could come to love and want to be part of—forever.

She stopped for a moment, catching her breath. Below her, the gully cut back down the mountain to Argentum. Above, it climbed to the pass, to Indian Cliffs and its walls of petroglyph-covered rock. It seemed so familiar, but she hadn't been there since that night . . . was it only a month ago?

She rather wished Jimmy were with her now. But when she'd asked him, he'd said he definitely preferred the practical to the visionary, and that anyway, this was hers. The stones had probably chosen her for a reason. After all, if the spirits weren't selective, Potty Pete would have gotten their message when he first picked up that stone in the desert.

Besides, Jimmy had said, he was now busy proving himself an eminent scholar in the job Kate's mom had given him in the museum. He had an uphill fight ahead of him, showing his parents that archaeology could be as honorable and lucrative as running a restaurant. But in the end, he'd win. Kate smiled. She had no doubt about that. He was one determined kid.

She started climbing again, boots scraping rhythmically on the gravelly earth. Well, alone or not, this had to be done, and she'd put it off too long already. Of course, there'd been plenty that needed doing when they'd first returned. One was telling their families a believable if highly fictitious account of an interesting, uneventful field trip. The next was giving the police an anonymous call about various illegal activities in a certain ghost town. But now there was one more thing.

The remaining stone wasn't driving her to it. Kate hadn't had any more visions. It was now only a carved Indian stone. But she didn't need visions to know that Wadat had lived to be a great shaman, and that in the end he had done what a shaman must do: He had trusted his soul, his charm stone, to the earth beneath his own spirit sign. She mustn't break that trust now.

At last Kate stood at the top of the pass. Between its cliffs, the air hung in calm waiting silence. In minutes, she found the boulder marked with three curved grooves. Kneeling at its base, she slowly dug out a hole.

Looking down at the scatter of dirt and pebbles, Kate suddenly thought of the eagle's view, and about time being like a river. All at once, she knew it was true. On one bend of the river, far, far back, Wadat and Hizu were together, leading their lives. And farther along was her father, happy with his wife and little girl. Her

135

eyes brimmed with tears. She wasn't sure if they were happy tears or sad, but she was glad they had come.

Calmed at last, she continued digging. But the silence had changed, and she knew she was not alone. Slowly she looked up.

A man, shadowy and faint, was walking toward her through the pass. She sat back and waited. He walked with slow dignity, and his hair was the color of pale gray smoke. Hizu?

As he neared, she knew it was another. The fine wrinkles on his face could not hide the three old scars. Carefully, he knelt beside her. Reaching into a worn leather pouch at his side, he pulled out a stone— smooth and red and marked with three curved grooves. The ground had been prepared earlier, and now he lowered his stone toward it.

She hesitated a moment, then gripping her own identical stone, Kate followed his example. The stones met and blended, becoming one. For a moment both hands held it, lowering it into the earth.

Wadat looked up, his dark eyes bright with recognition. "Spirit person, you are always where you are needed." He smiled. The dry air shimmered with heat.

Kate was kneeling alone beneath the cliffs. A fresh breeze had arisen, whispering among the pines, stirring dust in a glittering curtain. She stood up. It was time to go home.